Back Home For Christmas

Back Home For Christmas

AMBER REED

For my wonderfully supportive family

Contents

Chapter One

"What the…" I said, stopping myself just before the curse left my lips. I stood in stunned silence in the doorway to my childhood kitchen that hadn't been updated since the early 2000s and still had the rustic roosters to prove it. My cheeks flushed red as I remembered my frumpy plaid pajama pants, my braless, ribbed, well-worn tank, and my disheveled hair, fresh from being destroyed by a pillow, as the man who I had spent the last fifteen of my twenty-two years on the planet hating, eyed me up.

Just last night, I vowed to put on my happy face for Christmas despite not wanting to be there, but his presence in my kitchen tore that to shreds. He sat casually on the corner of a stool at our island where I once upon a time shoveled spoonfuls of Captain Crunch into my face before rushing to catch the bus. One hand held a steaming cup of coffee, while the other scrolled his phone. He wore a tight-fitting shirt and a pair of Christmas pajama pants. The combination of which highlighted a tapered waist and trim, muscular biceps. He stared at me with his piercing hazel eyes. One eyebrow lifted as if he had any right to be surprised by my presence. I felt judgement wafting off him like the stench of two-day-old milk left to rot. He didn't say a word. He didn't crack a smile or even nod his head in greeting. He just stared at me as I floundered, trying to make sense of it all.

"Morning Kitty Cat, sleep well?" He asked, after we both took several seconds to appraise each other.

"What are you doing here?"

"Drinking coffee," he said, as if he never spoke to someone so stupid before. "Would you like some?"

My heart pounded as I tried to slow my breath and not commit murder in the kitchen. After another heartbeat of waiting for something, anything, but preferably an explanation, I threw up my arms, huffed out a breath, and turned tail to run back upstairs. I pulled out my phone and texted Jenna.

> OMG! I have to talk to you! Coffee, please.

Morning to you too. Yes, I would love to meet for coffee. The usual place?

> Yes. See you in 5

I grabbed an elastic and pulled my long, straight black hair into a messy bun while sliding my feet into my fluffy, multi-purpose inside/outside slippers. As I reached for the door, I thought better of it and put a sports bra on under my tank, then I rushed back down the stairs as quickly as I had gone up them. I pulled my long puffy black coat off the hanger by the door before leaving, closing the door with more force than was strictly necessary.

Once outside, the cold winter air caught me in the face, making it hard to breathe. I waited a second to adjust before I walked down the porch covered in twinkling Christmas lights onto the lawn, overflowing with decorations.

For a few years, I tried to find the strangest, least Christmas like decoration I could and sneak it in with the overflowing yard to see if my parents questioned the goblin wearing a Santa hat or the half-naked woman with blinking lights for tassels, but they never did. My collection of Christmas oddities just got swallowed, finding their way back out front each year without question. For all their faults, I kind of appreciated that about my parents. All of my Christmas misfits became part of the family.

Once my body had woken up enough, I started speed walking to the coffee shop. I had lived in Cape Shore my whole life, so the habit of walking just about everywhere, except the cheaper grocery store outside of town, was deeply ingrained. When I moved out for college, I had looked at universities that didn't require a car. I found one with lots of walkability, but hadn't been prepared for the sheer size of the campus. It felt overwhelming for the first year, but now that I was back home after four and a half years, Cape Shore felt downright tiny. Although, I guess it always had been. The one thing I missed and didn't realize until I had stepped out of the car last night was the smell of the ocean on the air. I had yet to find a replacement for that.

Christmas was huge in town. Summer may have been the biggest boom in tourism and sales, but Christmas was a close second. The shop owners and local residents went all out with the street fair, parades, and a town wide Christmas party on Christmas Eve. I hadn't seen it in years, and I had to admit it warmed even my frozen over heart.

The Magic Cafe, while uniquely named, had been a staple through my formative years. There wasn't a chain coffee place for miles outside of our quaint beach town. It would have ruined the aesthetic and feel, plus I didn't think anyone would have gone there since we were all staunch supporters of local businesses. More than half of the locals owned shops of their own that depended on avoiding a big business take over.

Our favorite spot was exactly what a little coffee shop by the beach was supposed to be. It had mismatched seating, a shelf full of well-read books and board games, large windows that let in the sun and a menu full of drinks you wouldn't find anywhere else.

Outside of the season, it remained blissfully empty aside from high schoolers looking for a place to be after school. During the on-season, the line could snake out the door and down the sidewalk. People loved their coffee. I walked in, waved to Jenna, who had already gotten her drink and brought it to a seat, then I got in line. Luckily, it wasn't peak hours, and I got my drink quickly enough. The menu board was covered in chalk drawings of holly leaves and Christmas trees, and I couldn't just get a regular coffee.

"What kind of coffee is that?" Jenna asked when I sunk into the leather seat across from her.

"I had to get a peppermint cocoa. Don't judge me." Jenna just shook her head and held up her arms in innocence.

"I wouldn't dare." Although we hadn't seen each other much since I left for school, aside from an annual visit on her part, she was still very much my best friend and knew all the ins and outs of my life. I had met a lot of people in college, but I didn't connect to any of them in the same way I connected to Jenna. She was a part of my soul from now until eternity.

"Well, are you gonna tell me what the emergency was?"

I leaned forward over the table, and whisper yelled at her. "Jay is at my house!"

Chapter Two

"Jay Crowely? Why?"

"How should I know? I went to bed last night in a mostly empty house aside from my parents, and when I woke up, there was Jay, sipping coffee like he owned the place, and I was the intruder!" I took a careful sip of my peppermint cocoa. My nose dipping into the whipped cream before I scrubbed it with a napkin. I was in no mood for cute cocoa moments.

"Did you ask him why he was there?" She had the decency to sound adequately scandalized, but her question was ridiculous.

"Of course, I did," I said, my hands nearly slamming on the table as I leaned even further forward. "He is incapable of answering anything with a straight answer. He just gaslit me about coffee."

"Maybe he's changed?"

"Men like that don't change! It is pathological asshole

syndrome or something. I'm sure someone has written about it somewhere." Jay Crowely had moved into town when I was in first grade, and he was in third. He became best friends with my brother and mortal enemies with me, which sort of made sense since my brother and I weren't exactly bosom buddies. But still, he didn't have to go so hard on the make Cat's life miserable front. Eventually, I could go toe to toe with him, but it was never fun having to defend myself whenever Darren had his friend over.

"Is he still a smoke show?"

"A smoke show?" I giggled. "Jenna, please, I'm embarrassed for you." Then we were laughing in the full body way that only best friends can.

"I missed you. I'm glad you are home, even though you don't want to be here," Jenna said after the laughter faded.

"I missed you too." I sighed as I tried to take another sip of my decedent drink without getting covered in whipped cream. I should have just used a spoon, but I liked to get equal parts of drink and cream, so I couldn't just eat all the topping before I even got to the drink part.

"How was it? Coming back, I mean."

I shrugged. "Strange, frustrating, heartbreaking, wonderful," I said, feeling that same mix of emotions well up. "As much as I pretend not to, I love this tiny beach town where I can hear the ocean everywhere I go. But I also feel like a goddamn failure. Probably because I am."

"You are twenty-two, Cat. You still have time to graduate, get some hot shit psychology job, and rub it in your brother's face."

"Don't forget my parent's face too. And maybe Jay's now that he is around," I said. "Although listening to people bitch about their problems all day isn't all that glamorous." I had spent my childhood listening to my parents tell me, and anyone else who would pay attention, just how amazing my brother Darren was at literally everything he touched. You would think his shit was made of gold the way my parents talked. Darren learned to read at one. He knew his times tables by first grade. He was writing stunning poetry by second grade. He was acing all the tests by fifth grade. He took AP classes and got a scholarship to Princeton. He was polite, and handsome, and thoughtful. Meanwhile, I was just the girl who dyed her hair purple, wore doc martins, argued with teachers, got middling grades, and generally made people uncomfortable with my unfiltered existence.

I got into Rutgers by the skin of my teeth, but worked my ass off at two jobs, while taking as close to a full course load as I could. I hadn't intended to come home until I had finished my final essay, which I had to get an extension on, and graduation was guaranteed, along with possibly a job offer on the table to show some amount of success. Going into psychology had never been my plan, but my horrible luck and some amount of anonymous sabotage had left me out of choices and locked out of my dream.

I couldn't stand the thought of listening to all of Darren's accolades while struggling to get even a single one of my own, so I had spent Christmas breaks working and making excuses to not show up. I'm sure it only reaffirmed my black sheep status in my parent's minds, but I thought I would redefine myself when I had a six-figure salary and a bunch of letters after my name. It had been a silly dream; I guess. Especially since I couldn't even finish my final essay with the additional time. Every time I sat down, I felt lost. My ADHD didn't help, pulling my attention to easier, flashier things, but it was more than that too. With school essentially over, I no longer had a place to live. Had I known Jay would be staying at in my house, I would have lived in my car before coming home.

"Can't I come live with you for the break?" I asked Jenna.

"You know you can't," she said. "My parents have forgiven you, but I don't think they want you sleeping on their couch for a week, either."

"Jenna! You know it wasn't my fault! Who keeps dry potpourri around the base of a votive candle? That is an accident waiting to happen!"

"You are preaching to the choir."

"How the hell am I going to live with Jay for a whole week? I could just feel his judgement all over me when I walked into the kitchen," I groaned, letting my head tilt back.

"Is he really judgmental or do you just feel judged?" Jenna asked in her too wise way that was both amazing and incredibly frustrating when I just needed someone to bitch to.

"Who has the psych degree now? And no, he really is judgmental. It's like he thinks he is so goddamn superior to all of us. He looks down his nose at everyone, but especially me. If I didn't think Darren felt the same way, I would question their friendship. But to Darren, that's a feature, not a bug. He gets to be superior by proxy," I said, and Jenna snorted a laugh. "Did I ever tell you about the time in high school he convinced me that poison ivy was holly, and I should decorate the shop with it? When I got an itchy rash, he called me Cat Scratch Fever for an entire year."

Jenna snorted a laugh before remembering it wasn't funny at all. "Yes, many times," Jenna said.

"Fine," I said. "Anyway, what's new with you? How are things with what's his face from Delaware?"

"Over," Jenna said.

"Oh shit! I'm sorry. What happened?" I asked.

"Nothing happened. Nothing ever happens," she said. I knew how frustrated she was in her small-town life. Unlike me, she didn't get to leave, even for a college break. She went to community while working in her parents' restaurant. I felt bad bitching about having to be home for a week. Although, what I hadn't told her was that if I couldn't pass my final class, I would be forced to stay indefinitely without prospects for income or school housing.

Chapter Three

T he walk back to my house felt especially ominous despite the unbridled cheer all around me. By noon, the cobblestones of Main Street filled with tourists. I dodged around the mostly smiling faces enjoying the chilly weather, shopping, and general spirit of Christmas, trying to absorb their energy and force out my own dread. The Fred Astaire version of "Silver Bells," played over the speakers hidden throughout the pedestrian-only street. By the time I turned the corner of our little side street, I felt better. At the very least, I would have Jenna. I would spend my time hiding in my room typing away on my laptop or out making memories with my best friend.

As soon as I pushed open the front door, those positive feelings vanished as my plan to be mostly reclusive fell to pieces. My mother, father and brother all sat in the living room surrounded by ancient cardboard boxes labeled with some variation of Christmas stuff. While the outside decorations had been up for at least a week, they hadn't done much inside. I'm sure they wanted to make it a family bonding experience to cut down the tree and put up the ornaments and all that.

"There she is!" My mom said with a broad smile, holding up a familiar green and red striped smock with my name printed on the top left corner. When she looked up and really caught sight of me, her smile faltered. "Sweetheart, it's almost noon. Aren't you going to get dressed?"

"Sure, mom," I said, trying hard not to let my annoyance come out in my tone. She must have picked up on it regardless of my efforts.

"Oh, don't be like that," she said. "I just don't think it is appropriate to wear your pjs all day. And it's clear to everyone you haven't showered."

"The scandal," I gasped. "What will the tourists think?"

"Anyway, look what I found," she said, holding up the dreaded smock again. It was more than a smock, really. It was elf vomit in wearable form. The base was green and red, but beyond that it was a vast array of appliqué presents, bows, wrapping paper, and little woodland creatures holding Christmas gifts. With all the sewn-on patchwork, it made the once utilitarian work smock into an ill-fitting nightmare that had been my daily uniform for most of my life. Even in the heart of summer when everyone wore beach gear, I lived in that thing. Even in the fall, when everyone focused on spooky vibes, I wore the garish Christmas smock. It was one of the many tragedies of my early years that made me into the contrary pseudo goth that I was today.

"That's great, mom. Maybe we can make a little shrine to it at the shop," I said. I started walking past them, only to be stopped by her gasp.

"Absolutely not, Catherine. You have to wear it!" She said.

"It is tradition," Dad said with a shrug. I had intentions of grilling my family the second I walked in the door about why in hell Jay Crowely had been casually having a morning cup of coffee in our kitchen, but it was clearly too late. They were lost to the Christmas boxes and apparently had visions of reliving my youth with a pathetic fashion show.

"What tradition?" I asked.

"Wearing it when you work in the shop," dad said. Dad looked like a round teddy bear of a man, and most of the times he was, unless he felt overwhelmed, which happened with some regularity. Then he would bite your head clear off your shoulders if you breathed too loud. Sometimes I thought Darren took after him, but it was hard to tell because he hadn't faced a single hardship in his life, so it was anyone's guess how he would react to stress.

"I'm not working at the shop," I said. Darren let out a guffaw that left me rolling my eyes. He sat on the edge of the armchair opposite mom rifling through his own box. "What?" I asked. "Oh, and it's nice to see you too, by the way." I had been trying to move away from my default sarcasm as of late. It didn't go over well in the professional world, and I thought it made me sound childish, but what can I say? My brother brought out the best in me. I hadn't seen him in years, since he never visited me, and I never visited home, and he hadn't even greeted me. Granted, my mom could really dominate a room, but still. A hello would have been nice.

He stood then, tiptoeing carefully around the Christmas explosion, finding bare spots of hardwood to place his feet until he stood in front of me. He pulled me into a tight hug.

"Good to see you, sis," he said.

"Same," I said, with my mouth in a tight line. "You want to tell me about Jay?"

He opened his mouth to respond, but before he could, my mother was snapping a picture on her phone, then shoving the smock into my hands.

"Put it on, Cat!" she said. I rolled my eyes. I wasn't getting out of this, so I grabbed the smock, pulled it over my head, and held out my arms.

"There, you happy?"

"Oh! It looks great!" Mom said, tears making her voice catch with emotion. She held up her phone and took at least ten more pictures of me, that probably all looked exactly the same. "It will be so nice to have you back in the shop."

"Slow down," I said, holding up my hands. I wasn't used to the rapid-fire chaos of my family. "One, I am not working in the shop. Two, why was Jay Crowely here this morning?"

"Don't be silly, of course you'll work in the shop," mom said waving her hand dismissively.

"Jay's staying with us for the holidays like he always does," dad said, in his usual oblivious way. Darren had the sense to look down at his hands sheepishly when I turned my glare on him.

I took a deep breath.

"Hey Catherine!" Dad said. My parents weren't big on respecting nicknames. I turned to look at him. "Look what your mom and I found. We're gonna sell it in the shop." He held what looked like a bubble gun or something, but when he shot it in my direction, a strong puff of air and a loud crack sent little red, green, and silver paper confetti and glitter blasting over my entire body.

"Don, come on, now. Who's gonna vacuum that up?" Mom asked, as if she wasn't at all concerned with the fact that I had just been glittered bombed. Darren was giggling at my side while dad just smiled like he had won the goddamn lottery.

"Who is going to buy that?" I asked.

"Wow, you're really getting in the Christmas spirit," I heard Jay's voice before I could see him. When I turned, he smiled and laughed. For all the time I had ever known him, Jay had only ever laughed if it was at my expense. He stood behind me now, changed out of his pajama pants into jeans and exchanged his too tight pajama shirt with a too tight white t-shirt that perfectly highlighted his biceps, not that I noticed.

My life was like one of those sitcoms that I had to watch from behind my fingers or on fast forward or else I might simply die of secondhand embarrassment. Only I couldn't look away and the embarrassment was all mine. How I found myself back here at twenty-two was beyond me. Maybe it was just my destiny to be the butt of everyone's jokes.

"I'm going to take a shower," I said, spitting out little

pieces of colored paper. I would have to get both my brother and my mother alone to discuss the Jay situation and the shop situation, respectively. But for now, I had to get out of there as quickly as possible. It wasn't until I was out of the room that I realized I was still wearing the stupid smock that made me look like a rectangular Christmas gift. How did Jay always look like he stepped off the cover of GQ and I always looked like I had climbed out of a dark cave? It was insult to injury.

Chapter Four

In the bathroom, I let the shower run until the steam fogged up the mirror. I carefully pulled off the smock and the tank top underneath to keep as much of the glitter out of my hair as possible. I'm sure I would still find stray pieces months from now. The exhaustion of being around my family was creeping in faster than I had hoped. I studied myself in the mirror, silently trying to reaffirm my confidence and self-worth in the face of the demoralizing effects of my family. As family went, they weren't bad. I knew my parents loved me in their own way. I always had a good home and stability. But I lacked the support and unwavering acceptance that my brother got.

I tried to tell my reflection that I was more than the butt of their jokes, but it didn't ring true, especially when I looked like a clown covered in Christmas garbage. To make it worse, positive affirmations didn't help much to bolster my confidence when my life was days away from falling into ruin. If I didn't get my essay finished, I was stuck in Cape Shore until I figured out what the hell else to do with my life. It was the stupidest obstacle. I had gotten through so much worse, but somehow my mental block kept me from writing much of anything. I would be stuck in my parents' home, working at the shop until I came up with Plan B. It made me feel stupid for not having a Plan B in the first place. Although, I was probably already on plan C after the art school scholarship didn't happen.

"Get it together, Cat," I said, poking my finger into my reflection. "Don't fall apart." It was far too early to fall apart. I didn't know how, but I knew there was worse to come that I would need to withstand.

I stepped into the shower, letting the hot water run over me. When I got out, I felt a little better at least. I recommitted to not letting anyone get into my head. I wasn't a child anymore. I was an adult, even if I had to change course again.

I stepped out of the bathroom wrapped in a little green and red towel that mom loved so much, not for their utility at covering my body, but for how cute they looked hanging in the bathroom. My eyes were turned down as I tried to pull the fabric tighter, when I bumped chest first into Jay.

I looked up, face flushed, too stunned to speak as he towered over me, his broad chest filling my field of vision. I realized as we stood mere inches apart that I had never been that close to Jay Crowely before in my life. I felt like it gave me a new perspective, one that I hadn't been clamoring to have. Jenna's "smoke show" comment came to mind as I wondered how his tight t-shirt held together over his well-defined shoulders and biceps without tearing apart like the hulk. The scent of pine needles mixed with eucalyptus to fill my nose as I breathed deeply of his scent, entirely by accident, of course. Although it still left me a little light-headed and breathless. I'm sure that combination of manly fragrances had a powerful impact on most women. Not me, of course. He would have to do a lot more than smell nice to sway me. I realized my eyes roamed his body for far too long as I tried to pull my gaze away from his stupid muscles no one wanted to look at.

Our house was a hundred years old, and although our family had updated it several times, the upstairs hallway remained narrow between the four bedrooms and one shared bathroom. Jay looked down at me through his tussled brown hair as his gaze moved slowly over every inch of my body, bringing goosebumps across my exposed skin. My mouth went dry. I pulled my towel as tight as it would go over my breasts before steeling my expression and looking up to his face.

"You're blocking my bedroom," I said, my breath catching in my throat as I swallowed past the growing lump.

He laughed that stupid laughter reserved just for my misfortune as he turned to the side, waving his hand toward my door as if he was giving me permission to enter my own room. I rolled my eyes to make sure he knew what I thought of that before walking past.

I closed the door behind me, loud enough to reverberate through the hall.

> You sure I can't come live with you?

That bad?

> Worse!!

Yikes!

"Cat?" It was my brother's voice on the other side of the door, followed by a gentle knock.

"I'm getting dressed." I wasn't going to have a single moment of peace. I threw on some yoga pants and an over-sized hoody before pulling open the door. "What's up?"

"Can we talk?" I was tempted to slam the door, but I wanted answers. So, I pulled the door further open and waved him in. My childhood bedroom hadn't changed much since I left four years ago, and for at least a decade before that, aside from the teen decorations I had added over time. When I grew out of a toddler bed, my parents decorated my "big girl" room with pink walls, white furniture with flowers painted on it with a purple carpet, and they hadn't updated it since. I had a twin bed with a pink bedspread, a small white desk, a dresser, and a nightstand stacked with books I had intended to read before college but never did. Darren pulled out the plastic desk chair and sat.

"It's good to see you. I wish you hadn't stayed away so long." I raised my eyebrows. I believed him. As much as I felt jealous for my whole life, it didn't blind me to the reality that

Darren was a mostly genuine person. The eyebrow lift was because he must have known why I hadn't been home sooner.

"Why is Jay here?"

"Jay is my best friend."

"So?"

"So, he had nowhere to go for the holidays. He has been coming here since he graduated from college. Something you would know if you were around," Darren said.

"Seriously?" I asked.

"Yes. As soon as we graduated, his parents sold the house and moved away. They've been jet setting ever since without much interest in seeing Jay," he said. If I was supposed to feel bad for my high school bully after this sob story, it wouldn't work. "I know you guys didn't always get along, but he doesn't have anywhere else to go."

"'Not get along,' is an understatement," I said, crossing my arms over my chest.

"Tell me what's going on with you," he said.

"Nothing," I said. "Nothing new anyway."

"You still doing the psychology thing?"

"Yep."

"How's it going?" He must have known what a sore subject it was for me. Everyone knew that my four-year degree should have ended months ago. I knew he was just doing the brotherly thing of checking in, but it was the last thing I wanted to talk about.

"Alright," I said. "How's running Mom and Dad's shop?"

He cleared his throat. "Great."

I nodded. Of course it was. After getting his BA plus master's in business marketing, Darren had moved back home to bring The Winter Wonderland into the 21st century with an online shop to broaden their reach and improve profits. Just another reason he was the favorite.

"Is mom really going to make me work this week?" I asked.

He looked at me with a knowing expression, as if the answer was obvious. I groaned. "You know I have to finish an essay this week."

He shrugged. "Tell it to mom."

"I thought you were in charge now."

"I'm just the money and marketing guy," he said, holding up his hands. I fell back on the bed, staring up at the Billie Eilish and Lana Del Ray posters from when I fancied myself an emo pop girlie. "Not like the other girls," I thought to myself. But here I was, more like "the other girls" than the other girls themselves. That didn't make any sense, but I understood what I meant—there was nothing special or unique about me. I used to cling to my weirdness like a goddamn suit of armor, only to realize in my early twenties that I only ever wanted to be liked and valued. I sighed.

"That's a big sigh," Darren said, standing and patting my knee. "I'll leave you to your wallowing, but don't be long. There's much to do."

When the door closed, I didn't move for at least five minutes, taking deep breaths and dreading what would inevitably come next. I picked up a discarded crocheting project that I must have started before I left home and didn't bother to bring with me. I smiled as I ran my fingers over the chunky red and green knit, I knew would make a coffee cozy once finished. Before leaving home, I had just picked up the hobby, with aspirations of selling my Christmasy wares in the store. I could make hats, scarves, gloves, coffee cozies, plush toys, and everything could have Cape Shore or Winter Wonderland embroidered on it. When my photography had crashed and burned, I looked for a new creative outlet.

I knew it wouldn't make me much income, but to my stressed-out teenage brain, it sounded like a lot of fun. Of course, my parents had gently shit on the idea like they did with all things. Asking things like, "Are you sure you can make them look professional?" "Will it be worth your time?" "How much could we really charge?" Once those subtle digs kept coming, the crocheting didn't have the same allure.

My fingers moved with muscle memory as I picked up the project now. I didn't have to sell my coffee cozy to enjoy it. So, I let my mind wander as my hook moved in and out of the loops over and over. I thought about my photography. I had really thought there was a future there. Unlike my crochet work, I had consistently sold framed photographs at the shop. All of them beach or holiday themed that the tourists seemed to eat up. I tried not to think about it often because it broke my heart all over again every time it came to mind.

"Catherine!" My mom's voice came up the stairs as if she stood right next to me. "How long are you staying up there?"

"Coming," I said, finishing the little project and stuffing

it into the pocket of my leggings. I pulled my oversized sweater off and put on a bra and a red and green Christmas cable knit crop on, and traded my yoga pants for jeans. Maybe if I dressed the part, my mom would forget about the smock.

Chapter Five

"Come on," she said. "I don't remember you always being this slow. What did college teach you?"

"That the slower I go, the less I have to see anyone?"

"Catherine," my mother said with a warning tone. "Your father and brother are already at the shop. You know this is the busiest time of year."

"And yet, you managed just fine for four Christmases without me," I said as I pulled on my coat.

"Not by choice. It still hurts that you didn't come back once during your time away at school. I really thought you were going to be home last June," she said, her voice loaded with judgement.

"I'm sorry, mom. I wanted to, but I was so busy with my classes and working."

"And how is all of that going?" Despite not coming back, I had talked to my mom nearly every week. She had a pretty good sense of how things were going, although for the last few months, I had stayed as vague as possible. "Your essay is due at the end of break, right?"

"Yes, that is why I should be doing that instead of working at the shop." My mom pulled open the front door and let the biting cold sweep into the living room. I pulled a scarf down from the top of the closet and wrapped it tightly around my neck and face.

"I think snow is coming! Hopefully, it will be a white Christmas!" She said, stepping onto the front porch and ignoring my last statement. She had a unique talent for only talking about the subjects she wanted to.

"Hopefully not before we get the booth ready for the open market," I said before stopping halfway out the door. How did she do that? Here I was making her problems my problems, talking like setting up the booth was my responsibility. I shook my head and kept walking a few steps behind my mom.

My booth design was one of the rare things that she and Dad had ever praised me for when I was younger, so inevitably it became my job every year. The open market ran for only a day, leading up to the Christmas Eve parade that traveled down Main Street and through the pedestrian shopping strip, which ended with a big town wide party in the Convention Hall. One day didn't normally make or break our season, but it was a pretty huge part of our sales. Each shop set up their booth along the strip, so tourists felt like they were walking through an old-timey Christmas market. It was a pain in the ass and we froze our butts off, but it brought in a ton of money, so setting up the booth in an eye-catching way to draw in customers was important.

When we rounded the corner and the storefront and wooden supports of the stall out front came into view, my heart actually warmed. Traitor. I wasn't supposed to be this happy to be back, but the store was like a second home. I had spent so much time there in my youth, and there was something magical about the warm glow spreading out from the storefront window set to "Last Christmas" by Wham! Someone had set up a little scene around a Christmas tree with a menagerie of assorted stuffed animals stringing lights, hanging ornaments and wrapping presents in the window. I was a sucker for Christmas, despite my cold, angry, bitter heart.

Mom pulled open the door, and we stepped into the evergreen and cinnamon scented store with a train chugging along a track in the ceiling, animatronic ballerinas, and blinking candy canes. It was garish and over the top, but that was exactly how I liked it. As much as I hated to admit it, I was like my mom in that way.

I walked a slow circle around the edge of the store, noting the small changes back dropped by the familiar staples from my youth. Much like the booth, I had had a hand in the decoration and design of the store. My parents appreciated my eye for the Christmas aesthetic that was just right in enticing people to buy little holiday trinkets in the high heat of August.

Now, there were a few places with bigger changes, where the uniqueness of our shop seemed to be replaced with generic standards of modern day shopping. As if we were trying to mimic bigger name brand stores with personality deficient products. I shrugged. It wasn't my problem, right? I was sure that Darren had a hand in that after his one size fits all marketing degree tried to teach him that one size fits all marketing sold products.

"Shop looks good," I told my mom once I had made a full circle.

"Thanks dear," she said. "Can you grab that box, and we will bring it out to the booth? There is so much to do out there." She pointed to a large Tupperware container that I was sure held the outside decorations, or at least some of them. I picked it up and followed her out.

Outside, the booth's skeleton had been erected in painted wood posts and a covered ceiling. There was a table stretching directly across the front of the booth between the poles.

"Wait, mom, this isn't set up right," I said, pointing to the table. "We can't have a table here."

"You'll have to talk to Jay about it."

"Jay?" I asked. It was so cold, my breath fogged in front of my face. "Why would I talk to Jay?" I didn't bother adding that I never felt the need to talk to Jay again in my lifetime. Even if I had to sit across from him at Christmas dinner, I vowed to judge him without speaking a word.

"Who do you think has been setting up the booth while you have been away?" she said, her eyebrows scrunched together like I was being dense.

When I took a second look at the stall, it made perfect

sense that Jay had been in charge. It matched him perfectly; cold, austere and unwelcoming.

"No Elf outfit?" I turned to see Jay leaning against the far side of the stall, bundled in a thick puffer coat. At least that was one small grace. I didn't have to try to avoid looking at his body.

"I'll leave you two to it," mom giggled as she went back inside. I wasn't sure if it was because of her alliteration or because she knew how much I would hate being left to argue with Jay by myself.

"Mom," I called after her, but she continued walking away, determined to be back inside.

"Leave us to what?" Jay asked, picking himself up from his casual stance and closing the distance between us. His eyes locked on mine, pulling my gaze up as he stood too close for my liking. Had he always stood this close to me? Or was he trying to intimidate me? Or distract me?

Chapter Six

"You set up the booth wrong," I said, turning my gaze from his intense stare.

"I don't think so."

"Yes, you did," I said with more feeling as I waved my arm toward the table.

"It's been working just fine the last few years," he said so nonchalantly, as if he didn't care one way or the other, while I felt my temperature rising and fists clenching.

"I understand that you don't know any better, but if you put the table that way, you have less real estate for display, and people can't walk in to browse," I said. "If you set up the tables in a half rectangle, then people can walk into the booth."

"No," he said, as if it was beneath him to explain himself. He had always been a man of few words, which sometimes helped, since I didn't have to talk to him. But other times it meant the absolute stone walling that I was dealing with here.

"No?" I said. "What do you mean, no?"

He shrugged. "We don't want people in the booth."

"Are you out of your mind? Of course, we want people in the booth." The song playing on the outside speakers had turned over into Johnny Mathis' "White Christmas." It was a jarring contradiction to the tense conversation with Jay.

I should have just walked away. What did I care about the booth? My thing was psychology, not Christmas decorations. But if I walked away, then Jay would win, which I couldn't stand for. He had been winning since I was in first grade, and he convinced everyone that I had a crush on him, so all the kids called me Mrs. Crowely for weeks until I cried, and the teacher put an end to it.

Besides, if I was being honest with myself, which was rare, I kind of did want a say. The booth was my thing. It was stupid to care so much, but still, it was nice to have some creative outlet. It was the one thing I was good at anymore, and Jay had decided that he knew better, like he always did.

It made me angry to the point of tears, or maybe heartbreak. I felt like a shadow of myself, fading into obsolescence. Everything that had once made me, me had disappeared piece by piece. Who the hell was I if I couldn't even design the Christmas booth?

He stood, still too close, towering over me, with intense, scrutinizing eyes that never seemed to leave my face. I shifted under his stare, not sure what to do with myself. As angry as I was, I struggled to meet his eyes. I didn't want him to see the emotion there when he didn't seem to feel a goddamn thing. He was arguing about the stupid table placement, but he didn't actually give a shit.

"Listen, Kitty Cat," he said as I rolled my eyes so far into my skull, I would probably strain a muscle. "If we set it up to let people into the booth, then we limit the number of people who can shop at any given time. It will be crowded and uncomfortable and people will pass us by. Whereas if the table is set up like a counter, then more people can pass by and shop. It just makes sense." Then he reached up and tousled my hair. He tousled my hair? I stood there with my mouth hanging open for several seconds as I tried to make sense of what the hell had just happened.

"Did you just tousle my hair?" I asked incredulously.

He shrugged. "It felt like the right thing to do."

"On what planet?" I asked.

"I thought it would ease the blow of being so terribly wrong," he said. I snorted. He was more insufferable than I had remembered.

"I'm not wrong," I said, lifting onto tiptoes to reach his hair, but instead, I lost my balance and had to brace myself with one hand on his firm, muscular chest. I looked down at my hand, practically radiating with the heat of his body, then back up at him before pulling my hand away like it was on fire. My cheeks blushed at the thoughts running through my mind that I would take to my grave. "I don't know if you have pulled your head out of your own ass long enough to notice that we aren't in New York City in some high rise, corporate America board room," I said, stepping back and trying to recover some high ground. "We are in a small, quaint beach town on the Jersey Shore. Our customers want small town feel. They want an experience. They want to step into the booth and have a conversation with the locals. They want to feel like they have been transported. They want unique, meaningful souvenirs that they can bring home and remember their trip. Once they come into the booth, they are more likely to buy."

He was quiet for a moment, and I thought, for just a heartbeat, that I had somehow gotten through his thick skull.

"It's sweet that you think that, truly, but you are wrong," he said. "How about this? I'll split the difference with you. We can set up the tables in a half rectangle facing out. You can design one table; I'll design the other. Whoever sells more inventory wins," he said.

"Wins what?" I asked.

"Respect," he said.

I rolled my eyes. I would have to stop doing that or else end up at the doctor. "I don't want or need your respect."

"Are you sure?" He asked.

"Do not act like you know me," I said.

"Of course, I know you Kitty Cat. I've always known you." He said the last part, leaning down and whispering into my ear to add emphasis or throw me off, which, of course, didn't work.

"And I know you. That is why I know you would never give me respect either way," I said.

"Fine, what do you want, then?" He asked. That gave me pause. What did I want from Jay Crowely? The obvious answer was absolutely nothing. The less obvious answer was to see him as thoroughly humiliated as he had made me through most of my life.

Before I could come up with an answer, Darren approached, holding a cardboard tray of steaming coffees. As he approached, his eyes darted between Jay and I. I wonder what we looked like from his perspective. Probably a woman ready to throw down and wrestle on the freezing pavement, glaring at a nonplussed man who could just as easily walk away without a care. I don't know why I let him get under my skin.

"I come in peace," he said, holding up the coffee.

"Thanks, buddy," Jay said, grabbing two cups from the tray and holding one in my direction. I really wanted to Bruce Lee that coffee right out of his hand. Not sure why he felt the need to get mine for me. Before taking it, I reached into my pocket and pulled out my new coffee cozy. I had no choice but to take the cup from Jay before slipping the knitted sleeve onto the cup. I turned the cup in my hand, admiring my work with a pleased smile. It looked so cute.

The smile fell from face when Jay's laugh bounced through the open street, bounding off buildings to amplify the sound.

"What is that?" He asked. My gaze burned fire as I looked at him. I was tempted to just ignore him entirely, but then I had to remind myself that he was the stupid one for not knowing a coffee cozy when he saw one. I couldn't let him get away with that shit.

"It's a coffee cozy!" I said, my chin up, defiantly. I saw

Darren lift his eyebrow out of the corner of my eye. "Don't you judge my coffee cozy too!"

"No one is judging, Cat," Darren said. "Do I dare ask how things are going out here?"

"Great!" I said at the same time Jay said, "Not bad."

"How far along are you?" Darren asked, leaning over to get a peek behind Jay and I. His tone had become more serious than normal.

"We will be ready," I said.

Darren lifted his eyebrow, showing his doubt without any words. "Listen, I know you two don't get along."

"That's an understatement," I grumbled before getting another chiding look from Darren.

"But I need this booth to be perfect. You both need to work together and not let your differences show up in your work," Darren said.

"Don't worry, buddy," Jay said, patting Darren on the shoulder. A look passed between them that I didn't understand. Probably some stupid bro code that was meant to take the place of real human emotions they didn't allow themselves to feel.

"You know I'm not getting paid right," I said.

"You're doing it for the good of the shop, Cat," Darren said. "As much as you pretend not to give a shit about any of us, I know you secretly still care. You used to live for designing the booth."

I rolled my eyes and took a peek at Jay's expression in the process. Was he preparing to make fun of me with the revelation of just how important the booth had been to me in the past?

"Of course, I care about you," I said. "I'm here, aren't I."

"Took you long enough," Darren said. The heart to heart from the night before turned into a distant memory with this new, stressed out, bitchy Darren. "Just do a good job and don't kill each other," he said, turning on his heels and walking back into the store. I made a face behind his back. When I turned, I saw Jay staring at me.

"What?" I asked, throwing up my hands wide, daring him to challenge me.

"Nothing," he said shrugging his broad shoulders in innocence. *There wasn't anything innocent about that man.* As soon as the thought popped into my head, it sounded a little dirty, and I felt heat creep up my cheeks. *Pull it together, Cat.*

Chapter Seven

We stood in silence for several minutes after Darren walked away. I was looking at my table, but my thoughts were on Darren's mood.

"So?" Jay asked, pulling me from my thoughts.

"What?" I asked.

"You never told me what you wanted if you win."

"You know what I want?" I asked, rounding on him. "I want to watch you squirm. I want you humiliated like you have never been before."

"Kitty Cat," he said, eyebrows high, eyes wide, and voice a low growl. "I didn't know you had it in you."

"What?" I asked, my cheeks burning as I picked up on how he had purposefully added innuendo where none was intended.

"I just didn't know you were into that kind of thing."

"You are an asshole." My voice came out breathy,

betraying my rapid heartbeat as my stomach tightened and my palms sweat. Why the hell was he having this effect on me? I had spent my entire life hating and avoiding Jay and now, after ten minutes standing in a booth together, I couldn't keep my shit together. The thought of him thinking of me in a dirty, compromised situation left me swallowing hard past a dry mouth. Ew, this was Jay! "I want you in the Christmas smock, covered in Christmas confetti, telling everyone that I am a far superior shop designer than you."

He thought for a half a second before nodding his head. "Deal," he said, holding out his hand.

"Wait, what do you want?" He was thoughtful for a moment.

"If I sell more than you," he said, closing the distance between us again. I thought for half a heartbeat he was about to say something that would leave me blushing, or worse. "I want you to give me one of your old photographs."

"Seriously? Why? I got rid of them all," I lied.

"Then you can take a new one," he said. "I want a nice picture of the beach to hang in my apartment."

"Fine," I said, taking his hand in mine. There was no way I was getting my camera back out. I had given that up as far too painful a memory, and I certainly wouldn't do it for Jay's benefit. He had enough money, he could buy a hundred pictures of the beach. He didn't need one of mine. As my fingers slid over his palm, I felt a little jolt of electricity as goosebumps rose under my bulky sweater. When I looked up, his eyes locked on me with a renewed fervor. It was the first time I had ever touched Jay on purpose. I pulled away and turned toward my table. I had to get serious.

My table was empty. I studied it, hoping for some flash of inspiration, but Jay moving around behind me, pulled all of my attention. The booth felt tiny with both of us in it, especially because Jay was a giant. Every time he shifted even slightly, I felt the air move around me, sometimes bringing a whiff of his cologne. The constant reminder of his presence killed my creativity.

Setting up the booth had never been challenging before. I just went through our inventory and chose a theme. The goal wasn't to put out as much stuff as possible in order to blanket the stupid "market," like Jay seemed to think. It was about a feeling. The perfect combination of holiday nostalgia and lighthearted joy that his rigid marketing principals couldn't possibly manufacture. At least, I hoped it couldn't.

I lifted the box that mom had given me to carry out onto the table, refusing to turn around. I didn't want whatever Jay was putting together to get into my head. So, I lifted the top off the Tupperware and laughed when I saw the contents.

"Whattya got there?" Jay asked, standing menacingly over my shoulders. I slammed the Tupperware lid down. Not sure why I cared if he saw the contents, but they were all the things I had used to decorate the booth the last time I had done it four years ago. With a sigh I lifted the lid again, feeling a little exposed as I dug through the contents with Jay watching over my shoulder.

There was a garland of plush crabs, seahorses and starfish wearing Santa hats, a lamp with Santa in a bathing suit, a string of seashell Christmas lights, and countless beach themed ornaments. I felt tears prickle my eyes. Had my mom remembered my theme? Had she thought I might want to use it again?

"Cute," Jay said in his condescending way. "You have your side all planned out?"

I turned on him, without realizing just how closely he was standing behind me. There was less than an inch of space as I wagged my finger at him, but just ended up brushing my fingers against his firm chest. I sucked in an involuntary breath as whatever words I was about to utter, evaporated on my lips. I tried to step back when my butt bumped into my table.

"Personal space," I forced myself to say, even as my body reacted to being so close to his. My hormones were traitors. They always had been. I had never had crushes on the "right" guy. Jay stepped back exactly one inch as he smirked at me, waiting for a reaction. If he could pretend not to care, then so could I. What if he wasn't pretending and actually didn't care? The little thought popped into my head before I could chase it away.

Chapter Eight

"I will have you know that I never repeat a theme. Even I am not that tacky," I said.

"You should stick with what works," Jay said. "Was the beach theme successful?"

"Yes, of course."

"Then you should incorporate it this year. It is important to keep fresh ideas without abandoning what works," he said, using his lecture voice.

"Thanks," I said, making sure to deepen my frown as much as possible, so he understood just what I thought of that idea. "I don't think I need advice from someone who uses a ruler to space out the Christmas Tchotchkes." His table looked like it was cooked up in a lab. Everything just so. He wasn't done, but already it was laid out with the same rigid lack of joy that Jay brought to everything in his life. Even in his selection of items, they were nice things because they came from our shop, but they lacked cohesion, personality, or charm. He had two rows of mugs, a case of gloves and scarves, some stationary. It was as if he had a checklist called, "things tourists buy," and he wasn't willing to stray from it.

"You need somewhere for the eye to go," he said, as if that were obvious.

"No, you need to create a feeling," I said. I was talking with my hands, like I always did when I got worked up, but with Jay only a few inches from me, my hand brushed over his chest, bringing my eyes darting up to meet his. His expression held something dark that reached across the small gap between us and caused my stomach to tighten. I had touched him more in the last five minutes than my whole life combined. I wished he would give me a little personal space. If I didn't know better, I might start to think he was doing it on purpose.

I felt like I had known Jay my whole life. I practically grew up with him at my house, but when I tried to dial down to specifics, I came up blank. He never seemed to want to go home. I knew that his mom traveled a lot, and his dad could be a hard ass, but beyond that, our relationship existed in passing.

"Yes, a feeling that they want to own the items on display. A feeling like the things littering my table are the things that will fill the hole in their lives. Our job as the designers of this space, Cat Scratch," he said in his condescending tone as I quietly raged over the use of my old nickname. "Is to answer the question of what is missing? Create that Instagram perfect image that will draw them in and make them buy."

Frustratingly, I didn't disagree with him entirely, which made me want to ball up my fists and punch him. But the way he described it was so cold and austere. I had a different way of getting approaching customers to spend their hard-earned money. I wanted to provide something for them that they wouldn't get otherwise.

"I think it is really tacky to turn my parent's store into a consumerist money grab," I said.

"It is a store, Kitty. Of course, it is about consumerism," he said. "I may be in the finance industry now, but I got my undergrad in marketing and spent enough time in that world to know. It's all about the four P's of marketing; product, price, placement, promotion. The feelings come in only to satisfy those four things."

"No, it isn't. If you think that this store is just about making money, then you don't know my parents at all, and you shouldn't be anywhere near this booth," I said.

He lifted his eyebrows and looked at me with pity.

"Don't," I said, holding up a finger and waving it threateningly in his face. He had several inches, if not a full foot, of height on me, so I had to stretch my arm a bit. I watched as he almost smiled, which only made my own lips dip further into a frown. I let out a little growl. "Do not pity me. Do not patronize me and absolutely do not laugh at me."

His full lips formed a line with great effort on his part as he nodded. "I'll do my best," he said. "But..."

"Nope!" I waved my finger again, but he enclosed my hand in his large fist and pushed it back down between us without releasing my gaze. He didn't let go of my hand until it was firmly at my side. *What the fuck is going on?* I thought.

I needed to walk.

I turned on my heels without a word to Jay and headed out of the booth, but then I wasn't sure where I wanted to go. The chill in the air did feel like the precursor to snow and my fingers, which had burned where Jay held them, were starting to feel numb without gloves. So, I turned into the shop. Maybe I would find some inspiration there.

The warmth hit me like a wall, and I let myself relax just a little. I walked the shop and thought about nostalgia, joy and what made Christmas so special to me. Some people would say family, but for me, that wasn't the whole picture. There was an innocence to it, an anticipation. If I had answered that question four years ago, it would involve magic and creativity and my photography, but I worked hard to wall off that whole part of myself. If Jay could hear my inner dialogue at that moment, he would laugh and tell me I was over thinking it, or at least thinking about it in the wrong way.

Ugh! Why was I letting him get to me? I hated that he had that power over me. How the hell would I get through the next few days? I was supposed to be focused on my essay. It was my one and only ticket to a real life, a life away from the crazy of my family or the shop or the mediocrity that everyone expected of me. I had worked so hard just to come to the end and find myself unable to finish. Before settling on a predictable and stable life of psychology, I had all kinds of dreams that I followed with ardent dedication. No matter how much my parents had told me there was no money or future or safety in photography, I ignored them. There was rarely a moment without a camera in front of my face. I took pictures of everything, but my biggest inspiration was the beach with my parent's shop being a close second. It was the last time I had felt like myself.

When my entries for the scholarship contest had been defaced, a little piece of me died. My chance at a scholarship vanished instantly, but more than that, my ability to withstand my parent's constant brow beatings around my ambitions and a practical future crumbled. I put my camera away and never took it out again. I tried to get excited about the prospects of going off to college, getting a degree, and finding independence, but that high didn't last long as the grueling reality of paying my way through school set in.

Somewhere along the way, my ticket to freedom felt more like a prison. Self-doubt and imposter syndrome became my constant companions as I found myself shying away from challenges and struggling to complete assignments.

I had to face the possibility that shutting down and giving up was just my M.O. Because now, I had that same knot of doubt in my stomach as I thought about the booth, something that had come so easily and carefree only four years ago, felt like a monumental task. Was this what it meant to be an adult? Crippling self-doubt and an inability to get anything done? If so, I didn't think it was for me.

"You seem pretty mad at those Christmas ducks," Jay said, making me jump out of my skin with a shriek.

"Jesus Christ!" I shouted. Somewhere in my depressive

self-pity spiral, I had stopped in front of a display of Christmas rubber ducks. I must have been scowling at them as I thought through all of my issues.

"Shhhh, he'll hear you," Jay said, pointing to little baby Jesus in a manger display. My lips threatened to pull into a smile before I put a stop to it. Alright, that was kind of funny, but I wouldn't give Jay the satisfaction!

"Why are you following me?" I asked.

"I'm not following you. I am working on my display, and I was worried you might murder some ducks, so I thought I should step in."

"No, not ducks. Just you," I said with a scowl, but it only seemed to amuse him more. Why was he always laughing at me? I shook my head. "I'm taking a break."

Chapter Nine

My break turned into taking the rest of the evening off. I walked the shops from one end to the other, trying to recapture the feeling I always got as a kid at that time of year. Letting the lights, music, and joyful shoppers fill my soul with a little hope and happiness. When I was younger, it had been so much easier to let go. The stars seemed to align, giving me a sense of both self and purpose that I hadn't been able to reclaim since.

I felt better by the time I had finished my walk, as I made a silent promise to myself to reconnect with whatever spark remained inside of me that guided my passions, although I was nowhere near ready to take pictures again, I would finish my essay, design the booth, impress my family and show up Jay. I had visions of Jay standing dumbfounded, his mouth hanging open in shock and awe at the pure genius of my booth design. It was silly, but it made my steps a little lighter, and left me feeling like maybe, just maybe, I could pull it all off. There was still hope.

When I got home, the smell of burning pine and cedar met me before I even walked up the front steps as smoke plumed from the chimney. The familiar warmth of home and Christmas bolstered the hope I had fostered on my walk. Inside, I unwound my scarf, hung up my coat, and pulled off my boots. "Santa Claus is Coming to Town," by Bruce Springsteen played over the ancient speaker system in the living room. A fire crackled, the tree lights twinkled, and the smell of something comforting and delicious drifted from the kitchen. I teleported back to the best moments of my upbringing as I curled up on the couch, letting all of my problems melt away.

I turned on the TV, flipping through the channels like I used to do. My parents had most of the streaming services but hadn't been able to cut the cord with cable. So, I could still turn on the Hallmark Channel and watch a sappy Christmas movie, which played twenty-four seven so close to Christmas. They were playing *Serendipity*, which was one of my favorites. It brought me instantly back to my childhood when my mom would watch it with teary eyes on repeat along with *Love Actually*, *The Holiday* and a couple of classics like *It's a Wonderful Life* and *Miracle on 34th Street*. Mom, like me, had a tendency to prefer sappy romances. John Cusack wasn't my favorite love interest. I normally got weak in the knees for Collin Firth, but likely that was because of my love of the 1995 *Pride and Prejudice*.

"What I don't get," Jay's voice broke through my peace like a rock through a windowpane.

"Everything," I grumbled. He stood behind the couch with his hands in his pockets, stripped off his heavy coat, so his tight t-shirt could show off his muscles again, equipped with those sexy veins guys sometimes had. Before answering, he came around the front of the couch and sat down on the far end, where I had stretched out my feet, so I could lie down. I had to pull them up tight against me before he put his whole-body weight on them.

"Maybe," he said with a shrug.

"What don't you get?" I asked, although I just wanted to stay in my little holiday romcom bubble where everything can be solved with a smart little quip.

"Why it is romantic for her to bet on her current relationship to fail," he said.

"That isn't what she is doing," I said.

"It definitely is," he said. Serendipity was about two people trying to buy the same pair of gloves when they felt a connection, but she was already in a relationship, so she wrote her number and stuck it in a random book, with the understanding that if he ever found it, then they were fated to be together. "She is in a relationship and gives her number to another guy."

"Not exactly."

"All holiday romances are the same," he said. "What was that one you used to watch on repeat?"

"The Holiday?"

"Yes, that one. So dumb to think that two women would uproot their lives for men."

"If it was the right man, they would. If it was early 2000s Jude Law they would," I said. "How do you know anything about holiday romcoms, anyway? Are you a secret romcom fan?"

"You were always watching them," he said. I turned to look at him. It was true, for about a year there, they were my whole personality. But how the hell did he know that I was always watching them?

"They are probably the best love stories ever told."

"I didn't take you for a love story type of girl."

"You don't know anything about me," I said, feeling annoyed that he had encroached on this rare peaceful moment in which my brain wasn't sabotaging my own happiness. He was, in fact, very wrong about me not being a love story type girl. Before I became so jaded by myself and life, I used to love old love stories. I was a total sucker for a happy ending, or grouchy guy turned sap like in Pride and Prejudice or opposites attract like Ten Things I Hate about You. But the one I related to most was the self-sufficient but deeply insecure woman, learning how to let someone in like Breakfast at Tiffany's—problematic racist portrayals aside. When I dwelled on it, I got sad that my life wasn't more like the sappy movies. But I also didn't want or need a man to save me. I just needed to pick myself up and get my shit done. "Don't you have somewhere to be?"

"No." I couldn't tell if he was too dense to take the hint

or purposefully ignoring it. Either way, my foot itched to kick him right in the ass.

"You know, some people have told me that I look like Jude Law," he said, arching an eyebrow in my direction. He felt like a child acting out for attention.

"Only with more muscles," I said before clamping my hand over my mouth, my cheeks burning with warmth. Why would I say something like that? Now he will think I am staring at his muscles. And while sometimes I simply can't help it, the last thing I wanted was for him to know about it. He had a giant ego already. "I do not look at your muscles."

"I get it. They are hard not to admire," he said as he flexed his biceps and brought it up to his lips. Gross. *What an asshole*, I thought, letting my foot move down the couch and nudge the side of his hip. "Ow."

"What are you two doing?" Darren's voice came from the front door right before the gust of cold wind hit me.

"Close the door!" Darren swung his hand behind him with such force that the door slammed shut with a reverberating thud. "You okay?"

"What's going on with the booth?" He asked.

"Nothing."

"It's not done."

"We have another two days," I said. "What is going on with you?"

"Nothing," he said, forming his lips into a tight, thin line. I lifted my eyebrows with skepticism.

Chapter Ten

I took Darren's entrance as my cue to leave. I didn't need to spend any more time with Jay than was absolutely necessary, and I didn't need him shitting on my romcoms. I found myself upstairs, staring at my computer screen to no avail, before giving up and going to bed.

The next morning, I slept in to avoid seeing anyone. It was nice having the house to myself. I took a long shower, drank my coffee at the island and generally enjoyed my own company. I shared my apartment at school with two other girls, and although we each had our own tiny rooms, we were always on top of each other. Being alone was a novelty.

Eventually, I couldn't put off going to the booth any longer. I bundled up and headed out, only to find Jay already there. As soon as I saw him, I turned on my heels and walked into the shop, determined to ignore him. As soon as the door closed behind me, it opened again as Jay stepped through.

I let out a quiet sound of disapproval before walking the

shop for inspiration. It wasn't a large shop, but still big enough that if Jay wanted to leave me alone, he could. Instead, he seemed to be in every aisle right behind me. I headed to the supply closet that housed old merchandise and decorations. An idea had started to develop, and I wanted to see what kind of stuff we had.

"Can you please stop following me? I don't think it is fair that you are breathing down my neck as I am gathering things for my display. Wouldn't want you copying!"

He laughed. "I don't need to copy you."

His laughter died on his lips as I opened the storage room door and he gaped at something just over my head. I turned, and my mouth hung open. I blinked several times to make sure I was seeing what I thought I saw.

"What the...?" I said. This Christmas was full of surprises.

Darren looked up with wide eyes and bright red cheeks. His arms were wrapped around a beautiful blonde, wearing a spaghetti strap tank top and bright blue shiny leggings. I let out an audible gasp before I could stop myself.

"Aubrey?" I said before doing a slow turn to see how Jay was reacting to all of this. He cleared his throat as his face turned into an expressionless mask before he turned and walked away. I let the door close on my brother and Aubrey and hurried to catch up to Jay. Outside, "All I Want for Christmas," filled the street.

Jay was my sworn enemy, but he was the better option than the awkwardness we just left behind. Besides, I sort of, kind of, might feel just a little bad if that had been a surprise, especially if he had any lingering feelings for Aubrey.

Aubrey and Jay had been the "it" couple of our school for years. From my perspective, way down at the bottom of the social ladder, they seemed perfect for each other—vapid, stuck up, miserable. One day, they broke up, and no one knew why. To my knowledge, neither one of them ever spoke about it. Then they were off to college, and it was old news.

I hadn't thought about Aubrey in years, but I couldn't believe that she and my brother were hooking up behind Jay's back, or mine for that matter. Much like Jay, Aubrey had been a raging asshole for all of high school. Unlike the other popular girls who mostly ignored me, Aubrey went out of her way to let me know just how much of a total pathetic loser I was.

Once, I left history class with a bathroom pass, only to get to the bathroom and find Aubrey and two of her lackeys in there. She glared at me with a glint in her eyes as I ignored her and walked to one of the stalls. Before I could step inside, she moved in front of it, blocking my way.

"Sorry, this one's taken," she said. I tried to keep my face neutral as I moved to the next stall, but her little minions caught on and blocked my way again.

"This one too," the nameless girl said.

"This one too," the other one said. There were only three stalls, so I could either wait for them to give up and go back to class, or leave without using the bathroom.

"You are clearly not using the bathroom. Can I just pee?" I asked. I was a freshman while she was a junior. I couldn't figure out why she gave two shits about me, let alone hated me so much.

"Sorry, we are using these," she said. I spent far too much time debating what to do and arguing that when I finally turned and left, it was too late to walk to another bathroom. Even still, when I got back into class, my teacher yelled at me for taking so long. I still remember the embarrassment and frustration burning in my throat as I swallowed back tears.

Maybe Darren didn't know how awful she had been to me. Maybe he didn't care. Maybe that was why he had been such a tight ass since I got home. But even if all of those things were true, that still didn't explain why he would do that to Jay. I didn't care about Jay's feelings, but Darren sure as hell should have.

When I got back to the booth, Jay wasn't there. We had two days left to finish our displays, so it wasn't a big deal that he took some time off to collect his thoughts. For some reason, despite my better judgement, I found myself very curious what his thoughts were. I chalked it up to my inner gossip, but I found it distracting enough that it was hard to focus on the booth, especially since I didn't have the supplies that I had gone inside for.

"Cat, where's Jay?" Darren said, breathless as he approached the booth. I saw Aubrey behind him in a thick puffer coat, but she had enough sense not to come near me. Her eyes were looking everywhere but at me, which was a shame because I would have liked her to see the glare I directed at her.

"I don't know," I said as I pulled him further into the booth for more privacy. "What the hell is going on?"

"Nothing," he said. It felt like that was all we said to each other any more.

"When were you planning on telling anyone about this new relationship? How long has it been going on?"

He shrugged. "I gotta find Jay." He turned away from me and walked toward Audrey, who also tried to stop him, hands on his chest. I crossed my arms and continued my glare, ready for a fight. After a few more minutes, Darren and Aubrey walked away. I hoped they didn't run into Jay together. Seemed like it would be salt in the wound, although I wasn't sure why I cared. Maybe I just wanted a partner in my anger. Alone again in the booth, I had nothing to do.

I had to tell Jenna about this insanity. I could have texted her, but I assumed that she was at her family's restaurant, so I decided to just walk over instead. Jenna's family's place, The Lobster Tail, was the perfect mix of beach dive bar and the freshest seafood in town. Inside was all dark mahogany and wood paneled walls that made it look like I stepped into a time machine back to the eighties every time I walked in. Hanging lights and a few strings of Christmas lights, that Jenna probably insisted on, pierced the gloom. It was in between lunch and dinner rush, so only a handful of families filled the tables and a line of locals sat at the bar. One of which I recognized right away from his broad shoulders, although I wished I didn't.

Chapter Eleven

I stood in the doorway, debating if I could sneak past him to find Jenna. Of course, I could. Jay wasn't my friend to console. I didn't need to remind myself that he was just as bad as Aubrey had been back in the day. While he didn't have the opportunity to prevent me from using bathroom stalls, I felt like every time I turned around in high school, Jay was there. Even after he graduated, I felt his effects. Kids at school still told the stories of my many embarrassments or used the nicknames he had started.

And it's not like he apologized for being a total dick my entire life. He had done the opposite. Since being home, he had doubled down on the arrogance, obnoxiousness and teasing, treating me as if I knew nothing about my own family's store. Laughing at me constantly. Talking down to me. No, I definitely didn't owe him a shoulder to cry on. Not that he was capable of crying, or any normal human emotions for that matter. So, I shouldn't feel bad for just walking right past him. He probably didn't care about Aubrey and Darren at all.

With that self talk in my brain, I lifted my chin and started walking. I wasn't going to even look at him. I would pretend I didn't see him. Then I could duck behind the swinging door at the back and find Jenna to tell her the latest developments. I hadn't talked to her since I found out I would be setting up the stall with Jay and now Darren and Audrey? The news was burning through my veins.

But the closer I got to Jay, the more I noticed the slope of his shoulders, rounding down toward the bar. His head dipped heavy, his stare straight ahead.

No! I don't owe him, I yelled inside my head. But even as the words played on repeat, my feet slowed to a stop. What was wrong with me?

"Hey," I said, standing beside him. I would check in fast, then find Jenna. My butt wouldn't hit that stool.

"Hey," he said, looking over at me. There was an almost imperceptible shift in Jay's demeanor that I wouldn't have even noticed if I hadn't been stuck with him for the past day and a half. Still, I couldn't tell if he was sad or angry or something else all together.

"That was weird, right?"

"Incredibly," he said with a lift of his eyebrows for emphasis.

"I guess you didn't know anything about that either?" It was a dumb question. I would have had to be an idiot not to recognize the shock on his face when he saw them.

"No, I definitely didn't," he said. Now that I was

standing there talking to him, I had no idea how to end the conversation.

"Are you okay?" I asked.

He shrugged. "I'm fine."

I nodded. Was this my opening? Should I take him at his word and duck out?

"How do you feel about it?" He asked. Damn it.

"It's Darren's life. I guess it isn't really my business," I said. Points for diplomacy.

"I know how much you hated her," he said, and there it was. The statement that could draw me in.

"What?"

"I know you hated her."

"How could you know that?"

"She was pretty awful to you," he said.

"How did you know that?" I asked. Talking to Jay was a strange mix of surrealism and familiarity. He had been a staple in my life since I was in first grade always hanging around with Darren, playing video games in the living room, eating dinner, sleeping over, teasing me every chance he got, while at the same time I knew almost nothing about him. Until I arrived home two days ago, I hadn't spoken more than a few sentences to him. In these quiet moments, I realized he was at once a complete stranger and someone I knew so well.

"It was pretty obvious to anyone with eyes," he said. I found my butt scoot onto the bar stool against my will.

"If you knew what a monster she was, why were you with

her?" I asked, although I guess it made sense. They were both assholes together.

He shrugged. "I guess I had my reasons," he said. I scoffed.

"I'm sure you did," I said.

"That's not what I meant," he said, picking up on the subtext.

I made some sounds of disbelief, then we fell into silence. I was trying to decide if I wanted to hop off the stool and bail or force him to explain himself, when the bartender came over.

"Cat?" I took my eyes off Jay and turned to see Steve Turner standing on the other side of the bar with a hand towel hanging over his shoulders. "I can't believe it! I never thought you would be back here. All you ever talked about was leaving." When he realized who I was sitting with, his eyes grew even wider. "And with Jay? Have I stepped into the twilight zone?"

"Hi Steve, it's good to see you! I am not really here with Jay," I clarified. But then realized how shitty it sounded. Even if I did hate Jay, I probably shouldn't be outright rude when my brother had just stomped on his heart. Steve had been on the periphery of my tiny friend group in high school. Sometimes he was there and sometimes he wasn't, but I never knew who invited him. He also happened to be my very first kiss. It was awkward and unwanted. We were playing Cuphead on Steve's Xbox. It had taken us about thirty minutes to beat one level while everyone else partied around us. When we jumped up in excitement, he leaned in and kissed me.

"I mean, we are kind of working together this week," I said.

"I heard you were some big shot Goldman Sachs guy in New York City," Steve said.

"I am," Jay said. Talk about sounding rude.

"Cool, cool. So what kind of work could you possibly have back here?" He asked, oblivious to Jay's dismissive tone.

I looked from Jay to Steve, feeling unreasonably awkward. I didn't want Jay telling Steve the truth, that the two of us were setting up my family's booth. The impulse didn't make any sense. I didn't have anything to prove to Steve. There wasn't anything wrong with helping my parents while I was home, and Steve hadn't left our small home town either. He wouldn't think twice about the booth, and yet I felt so uncomfortable, which made me feel like a shitty daughter for somehow being embarrassed about my parent's shop. Or maybe I was just embarrassed that I was doing it with Jay. My feelings were all over the place, and it felt pointless trying to pin them down.

"I'm spending the holidays with Cat and Darren and their parents. Cat and I are helping with the Christmas shop." His tone was still so monotone, bordering on outright disdain. Did these two have history that I didn't know about?

"Very cool," Steve said, his perma-smile never faltering. "So Cat, what can I get you?"

I hesitated. Did I want to sit at this bar and have a drink with Jay? Was there anyway out of it now?

"Do you make those Irish coffees with Baileys?" I asked.

"For you? Anything," he said before turning to get to work. I smiled. It was cute, but when I turned to look at Jay, his scowl had deepened, which I didn't think was possible. Maybe he was thinking about Darren and Aubrey again. I wondered for the first time if he had some girl back in New York. Although, if he had, wouldn't she be here, or him there with her? Maybe he had a recent break-up.

"You know they make those everywhere. He isn't actually making it special for you," Jay said.

"Wow, bitter much?" I said.

A moment of awkward silence later, Steve was back with my drink. It was in a fancy little coffee mug with whipped cream and cinnamon on top.

"That looks amazing," I said. "Yum." As I licked the dollop of whipped cream off the top.

"Let me know if you guys want anything to eat. I can tell the kitchen," he said.

"Thanks," I said.

"No," Jay said. *Yikes*, I thought as I looked at him. He was staring daggers at Steve. What the hell was his problem? Was he just a total dick to everyone? And here I thought I was special.

"So Cat, how long are you in town?" Steve asked.

"I'm not really sure. I'll definitely be here through Christmas."

"Cool, we should get together, catch up," Steve said. "If

you don't have anyone else to go with, maybe we could hit up the Christmas party together."

"That would be nice," I said, feeling Jay's presence at my shoulder, making me feel as if I shouldn't even be talking to Steve.

"Cool, cool, I'll check back over in a few in case you guys change your mind about food," he said. When he walked away, I felt relieved, even though I had no reason to feel tense when he was standing in front of us. I couldn't decide if Jay's quiet anger was making me uncomfortable or if it was my own weirdness at sitting for a drink with Jay. I took a long sip of my Irish coffee and it was divine. I hadn't had one in so long, and now I couldn't remember why.

"This is amazing," I groaned, as I took another gulp. Jay watched me from the side of his eyes with an amused smirk as he took a sip of his beer. "You can stop laughing at me any time, you know."

"Who's laughing?" He asked. I sighed.

"You are, all the time. It's getting old."

"I'm just a happy guy."

"No you aren't," I said.

"How would you know?"

"Anyone with eyes can tell that you haven't been happy a day in your life," I said, my body felt all warm and fuzzy and when I looked at my drink, I had somehow finished half of it in the span of two minutes.

"Ouch," he said.

"Oh come off," I said. "Isn't that your whole persona?"

"I don't know what you mean," he said.

"Your thing is being pissy, bossy, too cool guy," I said.

"What are you Steve now? Everything is cool?"

"What is your problem with Steve, by the way?"

"I don't have a problem with Steve."

"Right," I said, shaking my head. I don't know if the coffee was already having an effect or if Jay was an incredibly difficult person to talk to, but nothing he said made a straight line.

"Hi," Jenna's voice right behind me startled me. When I turned, her eyes conveyed about a thousand questions as she stared a hole into my brain. "What brings you two in here?"

I remembered with a start why I had come into the bar in the first place. I hadn't updated Jenna about anything. She must have thought that I had been taken by the body snatchers if I was willingly sitting, having a drink with Jay. I tried to tell a story with my eyes, but I doubted anything got through her shock.

"Hi Jenna," Jay said. He turned in his seat, wrapped an arm around her shoulder in a half hug. "How have you been?"

"Same old," she said.

"Any movement in the bakery department?" He asked. She gave a small shrug.

"You know how my parents are," she said. What the hell was going on? Had she been friendly with Jay every year that he came to visit and didn't say a word to me? What a little traitor. And what was the movement on the bakery front? Had I been so focused on my own shit that she hadn't even bothered to talk to me about something as important as her dreams of opening a bakery? As much as I thought I was joking about the traitor part, it felt like a punch in the gut that she had this weirdly close relationship with Jay that she didn't have with me. Maybe we hadn't stayed in touch as well as I thought we had. Maybe never coming home had damaged the best, if not only, genuine friendship I had.

"I have to run to the bathroom," I said, swallowing back tears that threatened my vision. "I'll be right back."

I felt their eyes on my back as I hurried through the restaurant, feeling unsteady on my feet. Once the door was closed behind me, I studied my face in the mirror and blinked hard, willing the tears away.

Chapter Twelve

A minute later, Jenna was pushing through the bathroom door.

"What was that?" I asked, with a little too much emotion in my voice.

"I could ask you the same thing," she said. "Did you have a change of heart about Jay?" I shook my head and waved a dismissive hand.

"I just didn't get a chance to update you," I said. "I had no idea you guys were best friends now. So, when I told you that he was at my house, and you acted shocked, you already knew?"

"Cat." I had hurt her. "You haven't been home."

"That doesn't mean you have to cozy up to Jay!" Then a terrible thought occurred to me. "Do you...like him?"

"Stop being crazy. You always get crazy when you drink," she said. "I have no interest in Jay, and he certainly doesn't have any interest in me."

"What does that mean?"

"Nothing. But you can't expect me to hold up your personal vendetta for four years when he is here and you aren't. I have to at the very least be polite."

"That seemed like a lot more than polite."

"Only to you," she said. "You can't stand when anyone so much as looks at Jay."

"With good reason!"

She shrugged. "I guess. It isn't my place to tell you how long to hold on to a grudge, but you can't expect everyone to do the same. He's a pretty decent guy."

"To you. I've been home for two days and all he has done is make fun of me, laugh at me, talk to me like I am stupid and argue with me."

She sighed, "Then why are you here having drinks?"

"I didn't mean to be here. Well, I did, but I came to see you. My brother is being a royal ass. First, he is insisting that Jay and I decorate the booth together."

"Well, he has been doing it for years."

"A good job?"

She shrugged noncommittally. Which meant yes, she thought he was doing a good job. I shook my head. "Then we walked in on Darren making out with Aubrey!"

Now Jenna truly gasped. It was a relief to know that she hadn't secretly known about that too. "Aubrey Bates?"

"Yes, can you believe it?"

"Holy shit! How long has that been going on? Oh my God, how did Jay react?" She asked.

"Kind of like a robot, but that's why I ended up sitting with him. I couldn't exactly just walk by," I said.

"Wow, she does have a heart," Jenna said.

"I guess so. Who would have thunk it?"

"I'm sorry I have been friendly with Jay and that I didn't warn you that he had been here every Christmas since you left for school. It has been pretty lonely without you, and I still feel like I am trying to figure out who the hell I am and how the hell I should spend the rest of my life," Jenna said.

"No, please don't apologize. I'm being a dick," I said as I turned around and leaned my butt against the sink, crossing my arms over my chest. The bathroom was small with only two stalls and barely room to turn around, let alone fit two people having a heart to heart. "I haven't been totally honest with you. I know I told you that I am struggling with my final essay, but the truth is that it was supposed to be submitted before Christmas break. I couldn't do it."

"Oh no, Cat. Did they fail you?" She asked.

"Not exactly. She gave me an extension until January first, but it doesn't look great. Although my professor will accept it, I doubt she will give me a good grade, and that's only if I can manage to finish it. I don't know what my problem is. I have come this far just to choke. My self-doubt has finally suffocated me."

"Just because this one opportunity might not work out doesn't mean that you don't have others. You could take a semester off, then retake your final class. Or your could transfer somewhere and finish up," she shrugged. "It's not like your life is over."

"I feel like my life never started, and now that I am back here, I am worried I won't ever get out again," I said.

"Back here's not so bad," she said with her eyes down cast.

"That's not what I meant," I said.

"I know. But really, back here isn't so bad," she said. A woman with red cheeks, dressed in a glowing reindeer sweater pushed through the swinging door into the bathroom. She startled a little when she saw us chatting at the sink before she ducked into a stall.

"I gotta get back out there," she said

"I guess you don't want to save me from Jay, do you? Run interference?"

"Of course not. This is good for you," she said with a laugh.

"Asshole," I whispered.

"You love me." she blew a kiss and made a beeline for the kitchen while I slowly trudged back to the bar. Again, I could have just bailed, but my conscious wouldn't let me. Besides, I would just have to see him again at home or at the shop. I was living my own personal hell.

When I got back to the bar, there was a fresh Irish coffee waiting for me.

"Thanks," I said, motioning to the drink even though I wasn't sure I should have it.

"That was from your good friend, Steve," he said.

"Oh yeah, he's my bestie," I said, taking a sip to relieve the weirdness. The silence stretched again, each of us drinking our respective beverages, waiting for the other to talk. I wondered what was going on in his head. Was he hoping that I would just leave him in peace?

"Did you love her?" I asked. He looked at me like the conversation had taken an unexpected turn and he couldn't keep up.

"Aubrey?"

"Yes, of course Aubrey."

"No, of course not." I had an insatiable desire to know what "of course not" meant. Saying no was one thing, but of course not? That held lots of hidden meaning.

"What about you and Dan?"

"Dan who?" I took a long, slow sip of my Irish Coffee. It was criminally sweet, and I could have chugged it in two gulps.

"Dan Fletcher," he said.

"Oh My God, why are you asking about Dan Fletcher?" I asked. "I haven't thought about him in forever."

"I thought you two had dated."

"No, I had a crush on him. Everyone knew it, including Dan. One time, I was at a party."

"You? Went to a part?"

"Don't interrupt me," I said, pressing my finger to his lips. They were so soft. How much booze was in Irish Coffee? I wondered, pulling my finger away like I had burnt it. "I heard that Dan would be there, so I made Jenna go with me. Anyway, he asked me if I wanted to make out with him in his car. Just like that. No pretext, no flirting, just 'wanna make out in my car?'"

"Did you?" Jay's eyebrows were knit together as he leaned forward, waiting for the rest of the story.

"It was so stupid. I couldn't think past my stupid crush on him, so I let him take me by the hand, go outside and get into the backseat of his car. We were kissing, and I thought I was in heaven. Until his buddies pulled open the car door and tried to pile in like it was a big joke. Anyway, I found out that he had a girlfriend the whole time." I was quiet for a moment, lost in the memory. I had been embarrassed, but more than that, I had been so pissed at myself for being such a sucker. The older I got, the more I realized how hard it was to have any sort of self-esteem when you grew up with parents who didn't think you were all that great.

"Sounds like an asshole. For some reason, I thought you had dated him," he said.

"That's my life. Surrounded by assholes," I said with a knowing glance in his direction. "You probably thought we were dating because I talked about him all the time. I didn't really date anyone in high school. I tried to date in college. Well, I did date a little in college here and there, but I was too busy. I guess I always figured there would be time to date once I had established myself. Once I was worthwhile, you know."

When my rantings were met with silence, I looked up at him. He had his serious face on, which wasn't unusual. He was rarely not serious. But he also looked, well, kind of pitying. Why the hell was I sharing anything with him? I pushed my now empty glass away. No more Irish Coffee for me.

"But you and Steve were together, right?" He asked.

"Jesus, are you a stalker or something? No, just because I kissed Steve doesn't mean we were together," I said.

"Seems like he would still like to be together with you," he said.

I snorted out a laugh before covering my mouth. "No," I said.

"Yes," he said in the same no-nonsense way that he shut down other conversations when he was convinced he was right. It was the most frustrating form of communication I had ever experienced. It had a dismissive quality that made me foam the mouth to scream in his face.

"Some people are just friendly," I said while at the same moment another Irish Coffee appeared in front of me. I was already seriously feeling the effects of the first two. After freshman year, I didn't drink often, so two was enough to do me in. But Steve was smiling so sweetly that I smiled back, thanked him and took a sip, while Jay quietly judged me with his judgey, smirking face.

"What is your problem?" I could hear the slight slur in my words. I leaned closer to look up into his face, and nearly spilled off the stool before his firm grip wrapped around my forearms. At the same time, I reached out my hands and caught myself on his thighs, his thick, firm thighs. Time slowed to a stand still as my eyes met his, and my heart fluttered at the intensity of his stare. Maybe Jenna was a teeny tiny bit right about the whole smoke show thing.

"Whoops," I said, and then immediately wanted to crawl under the bar stool and never come out. *Whoops? Who the hell says whoops?*

"Maybe you've had enough to drink," he said.

"I'm fine," I said, slapping him on the chest. Holy crap, his pecks were firm. I pulled my hand away quickly when I realized I had been kind of sort of feeling him up. My hands had developed a will of their own, and for some insane reason, there will was to touch Jay. *Jay is an asshole who hates me*, I reminded my very naughty hands. *We do not want to touch him.* Then I giggled.

"Yeah, it's time to get you home," he said.

Chapter Thirteen

"Pfft, I'm fine. I certainly don't need you to tell me when to go home. I've been living there longer than you," I said. A full smile replaced his wry smirk and nearly took my breath away. I couldn't recall ever seeing the full brilliance of his smile. I almost told him that he should smile more. That thought brought on another bout of giggles, which led to Jay grabbing my upper arm and gently guiding me off the stool. The floor threatened to rush up to meet me as my legs wobbled precariously beneath me.

"Alright, I've got you," he said. I pulled my arm out of his grip with impressive force.

"I've got it," I said as I swayed over toward the stool.

"Sure you do," he said, grabbing onto my arm again. I stood on his right side while he held my left arm with his left hand. Then he slid his right arm around my waist. Goosebumps sprung up on my skin at his firm but gentle touch as he started guiding me outside.

The cold air that swept over me momentarily knocked me out of my stupor. I became cognizant enough to realize that Jay had his arms wrapped around me. I pushed him away, or tried anyway, because his solid mass barely moved, while I nearly fell on my ass.

"I understand that you can't stand me, but I would appreciate it if you could tolerate me long enough to let me help you home," he said.

"I don't need help," I said, to the accompaniment of *We Need a Little Christmas* playing on the street around us.

"Okay, fine, then do it for me," he said. His arm was still wrapped around my waist, and I was all too aware of the heat coming off his body and the feel of his fingertips where they pushed into my hip. I wanted to both murder him and see what his hands might feel like on my bare skin at the same time. It was confusing.

"I really do want to know what your problem is," I said as we walked slowly along the cobblestones. To outsiders, we must have looked like a very happy couple taking a stroll.

"What makes you think I have a problem?" He asked.

"Well, first of all, everyone has a problem. Some people are just better at hiding it."

"How very wise of you." I didn't have to look at him to know there was a smirk on his face.

"You, specifically, have a problem because you are miserable and hate everyone. We talked about this," I said. "I just want to know why."

He was silent, as if he was actually contemplating what I had said.

"I'm sure I have lots of problems," he said. It was the most introspective and thoughtful I had ever heard him. Maybe he had one too many beers, too.

"Maybe you just need to get laid," I said, then immediately clapped my hand over my mouth, which had detached itself from my brain and was taking my hands lead, apparently.

"Are you offering?" He asked with that stupid smirk.

"Ewww," I said, pulling away again, before he pulled me forcefully back to his side. I felt the length of my body from hip to shoulder pressed perfectly against his warmth, and before I could stop myself, I snuggled in closer away from the biting wind and into the crook in his shoulder. I heard his heart beat and the sharp intake of breath with my ear pressed against the side of his ribs.

I fell into a comfortable silence, listening to his heart and enjoying his body heat, forgetting who I clung to. I followed along through the streets as the Christmas sting lights fuzzed in my vision and the overall vibe left me warm and fuzzy. Before making it onto our quiet road, my eyes felt heavy when some delicious scent hit my nose.

"Is that you?" I asked, tilting my chin up and taking in a big breath through my nose. The pine and eucalyptus smelled intoxicating this close. I wrapped my fingers around his cable knit Christmas sweater and pulled him down toward me so my nose pressed into his neck. I felt his quick pulse against my skin as I breathed him in. We had stopped walking so we could stand on the glowing sidewalk with my body molded against his as he leaned down closer to me.

I felt as he swallowed hard. "What are you doing?" He asked.

"It smells so good." I pulled away, my fingers still curled in his sweater, regretting the loss of his warmth. When I looked up, he was staring at me from only an inch away. Without permission, my eyes darted to his lips, full and parted slightly. I looked away quickly and stepped back, pushing him away. My foot caught on a bump in the raised side walk, that or I was just drunk, and I tipped precariously before Jay pulled me upright, back into his arms. *I have to get away from this man,* I thought to myself.

"I've gotta get home," I said, shaking my head, somehow back in his arms. *I hate this man, remember?* I chided myself. And more importantly, he hated me. We were sworn enemies. He had made my life a living hell and just because he was walking me home, didn't absolve him of his past sins. I pulled away again, made sure I was steady and started walking up the path to the house.

"We are going to the same place. It is dark, and you have had too much to drink," he said.

"You aren't my brother. I don't need you telling me what to do." I turned and pointed my finger into his chest, which didn't give in the slightest. I spread out my fingers and let them move lightly along his chest. "Hmmm," I said.

"Come on," he said, grabbing me around the waist again and moving us forward. I made a quiet promise to never drink around Jay again. I clung to him as we stumbled up the stairs, well I stumbled, and he practically carried me. A frustrated sigh escaped his lips. It must have been killing him just a little inside having to help me. I wanted to pull away, but I had done that enough times to know I would end up on my ass on the frozen ground, so I let him drag me up the stairs.

The warm air hit like a welcome hug as we stepped inside, but didn't do much for my Bailey's induced sleepiness. I wanted to sink into the comfy feeling of home, but the sound of Darren's voice in the kitchen made my eyes wide. I wanted to talk to Darren before Jay got to him. I wanted a raw version of events rather than one edited to be more palatable. But I was in no condition to have a confrontation with him. I grabbed Jay's sweater again and made shifty eyes that I hope conveyed "let's get upstairs." But probably just made me look insane. He either got the hint or felt the same way about seeing Darren right then, and picked up our pace. The stairs loomed ahead of me and I giggled. This was going to be fun as I lifted my foot and missed the first step. I would have face planted if Jay didn't have a hold of me.

"Alright," he whispered before grabbing me roughly around the waist and throwing me over his shoulder.

I let out a squeal before remembering we were trying to get through the house undetected. The last thing I wanted was Darren to find Jay hauling me off to my bedroom in a fireman's carry. Speaking of which, what the fuck? Jay was carrying me up to my bedroom. I could feel his cheek pressed into my ass, and while the sane part of my brain thought it was the most mortifying moment of my entire life, the drunken part thought it was hilarious. I had to hold my hand over my mouth to prevent the laughter from drifting to the kitchen.

Jay walked up the stairs like I weighed nothing at all, and we were in my bedroom with the door closed before I had composed myself. He dropped me onto the bed, and I bounced a little, reigniting my laughter.

"Why are you being so nice?" I asked once my laughter had settled. He stood awkwardly in the middle of the room as if he didn't want to touch anything. He looked around like an explorer who had discovered some lost wonder of the world. It occurred to me through my stupid drunken haze that Jay Crowely was in my bedroom with the tiny twin bed and all the accoutrements of my teen years that he would likely ridicule me endlessly about, like my knitting, paintings and poems scrawled on loose leaf paper. That was embarrassing.

"I'm not being nice," he said. "I'm just being decent."

"Oh, that's right. Cause you can't possibly be nice to me," I said.

"I guess not," he said. I sat up and reached for my boots, but before I could get the laces undone, Jay kneeled in front of me. Suddenly, the humor in the situation vanished, replaced with the vision of this hulking, muscular man unlacing my boots with carefully placed fingers. I studied him, able to watch him without being noticed for the first time. I had the overwhelming urge to rake my fingers through his dark shaggy hair, and before I could stop myself, I was. He looked up at me, startled. He had pulled off my first boot and paused midway through the second one.

"What are you doing?" He asked.

"You have nice hair."

"Glad you like it."

"Why do you hate me so much?" I could feel his eyes on me, but I refused to meet them, instead focusing my attention on my fingers in his hair. He got the second boot off and lifted up high enough on his knees that I could no longer reach his hair.

"I don't hate you."

"Sure. That's why you tortured me my whole damn life." I didn't have a choice but to drop my hands and look at his face.

"You know, you aren't bad looking. It would be better if you were," I said.

"Why is that?"

"It would be easier to hate you when you are kneeling in front of me," I said. Fuck. His expression remained stoney. I let my eyes remained locked on his.

He cleared his throat. "Cat," he said. I was just drunk enough. I leaned forward and pressed my lips to his. They were warm, firm and tentative all at the same time before he lost any hesitation and wrapped his strong fingers around the back of my neck, pulling me tight against him. Kissing me with a fervor I had never experienced before. He wrapped his second arm around my waist and squeezed, forcing me to open my legs and wrap them around his body.

My lips parted slightly as he played his tongue across them. I was drowning, and I never wanted to come up for air. My whole body became pliable as he kissed me, sending shivers out to all of my nerve endings and making my brain go to mush.

He pulled away so suddenly, I almost fell forward. I opened my mouth to say something, but he brought his fingers to his lips to silence me.

"Shh," he said. Down the hall there were footsteps, followed by a knock on another door.

"Jay?" It was Darren, at Jay's door.

"Do you want to go talk to him?" I whispered, still pressed close to him.

"Not right now," he said. I nodded. He said he wasn't in love with Aubrey, but I had to imagine the situation stung a little. Hell, it stung me a lot. It felt like my brother was determined to only bring people who treated me like shit around this Christmas. Darren knocked again.

"Jay, are you in there? I just want to talk," Several silent minutes passed as Jay and I waited, my heart thundering in my throat, wondering what layer of hell I somehow found myself in. I had kissed Jay? And now my brother might find us? I needed a goddamn Christmas miracle. Miracle on Cape Shore beach in which Santa Claus climbs in through the window and stops me from making any more incredibly stupid decisions.

My stomach dropped as Darren's steps grew louder rather than quieter. Then his knock shook my door.

"Cat?" He asked. Was my door locked? I wondered with mind numbing panic. I couldn't move. I should have pushed Jay away and tried to act casual, but there was no casual with Jay in my bedroom.

"I'm not dressed," I slurred.

Jay looked at me with incredulous eyes, like it was the

stupidest thing I could have said, but I needed Darren not to walk in.

"Ummm alright, have you seen Jay? I need to talk to him.".

"Of course I haven't seen Jay," I said, while staring directly into Jay's eyes.

"Listen," he said. "Can we talk, about...you know."

"Yeah, sure, but not right now."

"What is going on?"

"I'm getting changed. I'll be down in a bit," I said.

"Okay. I think dinner will be ready soon, please don't tell mom about Aubrey. They won't care, but I just don't want to make a scene, you know," he said.

"Yes, fine," I said. Somehow, he chose that moment to have the longest conversation in the history of conversations through my bedroom door. My palms started to sweat and my stomach was doing flips. I might throw up. I might throw up right onto Jay's lap. The thought was both terrifying and hysterical. I had to bite back a laugh. It might be perfect pay back for the time he hid rotting eggs in my car after Easter. I swear I never got that smell out.

"Everything okay?" Darren asked through the door. His guilt must have been making him worried.

"I'm fine. I'll see you in a few minutes," I said.

"Alright. See you downstairs," he said. After the longest second of my life, I hear Darren's footsteps retreat.

Then it was just me a Jay. I turned my attention back to him, feeling my cheeks burning red. Only a moment ago, I was kissing Jay Crowley. It didn't compute in my brain.

"Cat," he said in a horse whisper, sitting back on his heels to put distance between us, clearly coming to his own senses.

"No, no, that didn't just happen. We will never speak of this again. We will chalk it up to the alcohol and the shock of the Darren/ Aubrey revelation. But we will not, under any circumstances, speak of this again," I said. I stood up abruptly, making my head swim. I rested a hand on his shoulder to steady myself before I pulled it back. "No more touching," I said out loud to myself.

He let out a quiet laugh.

"This isn't funny. I know my awkwardness is a source of endless amusement for you, but I swear to God if you use this against me," I said, not finishing the threat as my stomach acid threatened to come up through my throat.

"Kitty Cat, I think you need to take a deep breath," he said. "Darren is downstairs. We are going to split up and walk down separately and have a normal dinner."

"We can't go to dinner," I said. "Look at me. I'm drunk. And I just made out with you." I groaned and sat back on the bed, head in my hands, waiting for the mortification to pass. "I have to leave the country."

"I am going to go into my room. I will stay there until dinner time. Then I will go downstairs," he said.

"No, Darren was just knocking. He knew you weren't in there," I said, panic constricting my lungs. How was this my life?

"Take a breath, Cat Scratch," he said.

"You're an asshole," I said.

"I will tell him that I wasn't ready to talk, so I didn't answer," he said.

"I cannot possibly sit through dinner with you," I said.

"If I can sit through dinner with you, then you can sit through dinner with me," he said.

"You are going to tell everyone," I cried, returning my head to my hands.

"Why would I do that?" He asked.

"To embarrass me," I said.

"And myself by association," he said.

"Oh please, you aren't capable of embarrassment. Besides, kissing me is like one big joke in a long line of jokes," I said.

"I'm going now, Kitty Cat," he said. "I will see you at dinner."

He stood and left, quietly closing the door behind him.

Holy shit. Fuck. Fuck. How the hell did that just happen? I practically threw myself at Jay. What the fuck was I thinking? Hot tears slipped out of my eyes. He had been nice for all of two seconds helping me home, and I was climbing all over him. I stood up and started pacing the room.

I bet he only kissed me back because it was a novelty. Kiss the chick that you couldn't stand, see what it was like. Then he could use it as ammo against me for the rest of our lives. He probably made out with girls all the time like it was nothing. Meanwhile, I haven't had a boyfriend, let alone a good hook-up, in so long it was a wonder I remembered how.

I couldn't go down to dinner. I wouldn't. It was decided.

Chapter Fourteen

"Cat," Darren's voice echoed through the house. "Dinner."

I froze mid pace. I would tell them I was sick. Thirty minutes earlier, I had to be carried up the stairs. It made sense that I should just fall into bed and not get out again until I died and had to be carted off in a body bag, right?

"Cat? Are you coming?" Darren called up again. I heard Jay's door open, and his heavy footsteps go down the stairs.

I heard Darren and Jay's muffled voices, and I wished I could hear what words were being exchanged. Was it polite pleasantries ignoring the elephant in the room? Was Jay confessing that he kissed me? Was he yelling at Jay for taking his ex-girl? Was Darren apologizing? I wanted to know so badly, I almost left my room, but then remembered I had to pack my bags and move to Antarctica and didn't have time for idle gossip.

They moved too far away from the stairs for me to hear their voices. I imagined that mom was putting the serving dishes on the table. During the week leading up to Christmas, every night was like practice for the main event, with elaborate side dishes and fantastic mains. It was fabulous if you weren't confined to your room out of unrelenting embarrassment.

Several minutes later, a knock came on my door, and I shuddered. "Cat," it was mom's voice.

I opened it and peaked into the hall to make sure no one followed her up.

"What's up?" I asked.

"It's dinner. I know you heard your brother calling," Mom said, leaning in the doorway with her arms crossed, wearing one of her countless Christmas sweaters that could easily win the ugly contest. It was a familiar scene that she had assumed during so many of my talking-tos during high school. Why aren't my grades better? Why don't I take any honors classes? Why don't I volunteer more? Why don't I have ambitions like Darren? What are you going to do when you graduate? Photography won't make you any money. Why can't you be more practical like your brother? Seeing her like that only added to my anxiety. She only leaned like that when it was a conversation, I wanted to avoid.

"I'm not feeling great," I said.

"Well, a good meal will help you feel better," she said. "Come on."

"I really don't know if I am up for it," I said.

"Catherine, you are only here for a week. You will eat

dinner with your mother," she said. I tried very hard not to revert back to a sixteen-year-old who slumped and whined and rolled my eyes, but it took all of my effort, and left me vulnerable to coercion. "Let's go." She invaded my space, grabbed my arm, and dragged me down the stairs. My vision spun a little with intoxication aided by anxiety, as I tried to prep for the disaster I was walking into, but no matter how hard I tried, I couldn't think clearly.

Dinner was at the dining room table, a mix of high-end fancy, *Life and Style* and quaint, rustic, *Country Gardens*. The end result meant your eyes didn't have anywhere to settle at any given moment. Tall red candles in crystal holders sat in the middle around an elaborate poinsettia arrangement. The tablecloth was checkered red and green plaid with China plates covered in Christmas trees.

"Here we are," mom announced cheerily as she took her seat at the head of the table.

All eyes turned to me when I walked in, and my cheeks grew warm. I kept my gaze down. There were two empty chairs. One next to Darren and one next to Jay. *Pick your poison,* I thought to myself. I decided on sitting next to Jay. That way I didn't have to look him in the eye. My plan was to shovel food into my mouth as quickly as I could without barfing and run back upstairs to sleep for the rest of my life.

The scraping of my chair legs across worn out hard wood ground into my bones, giving everyone more reason to continue staring at me. Once I sat, I filled my plate with food and started sawing into the ham.

"Isn't this nice?" mom said as she grabbed a scalloped potato dish and started passing.

"It's very nice, mom," Darren said.

"Thank you for cooking again, Mrs. Lane," Jay said. "I keep saying that one of these days I am going to get you to let me cook a meal, so you can relax."

I felt my face shifting to silently mock his words as I scooped potatoes onto my plate, despite my goal to fly under the radar. When I passed the potatoes onto Jay and looked up, Darren was shaking his head in disgust. I shrugged and mouthed, "What?"

"You know what?" he mouthed back. I rolled my eyes. Now I couldn't even mock Jay? What was this world coming to?

"Don't be silly. You are our guest. Besides, I enjoy cooking," she said. Mom did not enjoy cooking. If you stepped foot into the kitchen at any point during her meal preparation, you would be screamed at and sent away. What she liked was the praise and recognition that came while everyone ate. She would never give that to Jay, no matter how much she liked him.

"Do any of you kids have a date for the Christmas party?" Dad asked and my wide eyes focused in on Darren, waiting to see what he would say anything. A moment of silence ticked by as I held my breath, willing Darren to say it so I could forget that Jay's elbow kept touching mine every time he scooped food onto his plate. The delicate hairs running along my arm stood up every time we touched.

"Cat might be going with Steve," Jay's voice startled me so much that I choked on my water.

"What? No, I'm not," I said at the same time Darren said, "Steve Miller?"

"Oh, he's a nice boy," Dad said, oblivious to the tension that pulled tight through three of the five people sitting at the table.

"I'm not going with Steve," I said.

"He asked you and you said yes," Jay said. As usual, I couldn't read his tone. Was he making fun of me?

"No, he said maybe we could go," I said. "I was just being nice."

"I don't think that's how he heard that response," Jay said.

"Wait, where did you guys run into, Steve?" Darren asked. I looked up. This was taking a turn that I didn't want it to take.

"The Lobster Tail," Jay said. Now I heard the smirk in his voice, clear as day. He was trying to embarrass me.

"Why were you two at The Lobster Tail together?" Darren asked. "Aren't you guys supposed to be working on the booth?"

"We've got it under control," I said. "You don't need to keep checking up on us."

"We were getting drinks," Jay said. Jay's words landed like a flash bang into the dining room, leaving everyone gapping in silence. Mom recovered first.

"Isn't that nice? I'm glad you two are getting along. I

knew the Christmas spirit would work its magic," she said. Darren's eyes narrowed.

"Why were you getting drinks?"

"I was there to see Jenna," I said, as if that answered his question.

"Oh how is Jenna?" Mom asked.

"But how did you two end up having drinks together?" Darren asked, pointing his finger between Jay and I.

I ventured a glance in Jay's direction. He turned to meet my eyes. I didn't know why Darren was pushing this because the answer seemed self evident. Unless, of course, Darren suspected there was something going on between Jay and I, which now that I was getting mildly more sober, there definitely wasn't.

"I guess we both just ended up there after stopping in the supply closet," Jay said, his voice full of implication. "Cat saw me having a drink and stopped over. And," jay shrugged. "We just had some drinks. That's when she agreed to the date with Steve."

"Oh my God. I didn't agree to a date with Steve," I said.

"Steve sure thinks you did." was he teasing me? Did he think that I wasn't good enough for Steve or that Steve was a loser? I couldn't figure it out.

"Who cares about Steve?" Darren asked.

"Cat does," Jay said. "Don't you care about your sister's love life?"

"It's not my love life!" I was almost shouting. Me, Jay and Darren had all been neglecting our food during this exchange. My parents watched the back and forth like a tennis match.

"Steve would like it to be," Jay smirked. Goddamn it. I had let him get under my skin again.

"You are impossible," I said. Although I guess teasing me about Steve was better than telling everyone about what happened in my room.

"I don't know why you two were at the bar, getting wasted when you should have been working," Darren said.

"Catherine, are you drunk?" Mom said in a very clutching her pearls tone.

"A little," I shrugged. "At least I wasn't making out in the supply closet."

"No, not in the supply closet," Jay said. I could feel my face turning red, and I was tempted to punch Jay right in the face, even if it might give away the meaning of his cryptic response.

"The supply closet?" Dad asked.

"You are an asshole, Cat," Darren said.

"Am I though?" I asked. "Cause I'm pretty sure you take that prize tonight. I thought Jay was your best friend. You always had his back when I came to you complaining, but you didn't seem all that concerned with his feelings today, or mine, for that matter."

"Wow, you are defending Jay? That's really something. But is it really Jay you are concerned about, or is this about you like everything else?" Darren said glaring daggers in my direction. I met Darren's pointy eyes and raised him smug condescension. Jay topped us all with emotionless indifference.

"I would like to have a nice meal," Mom said. "I don't know what is going on between you three, but perhaps we can put it aside for dinner?"

"Nothing is going on between *us* three," I said.

"I think the meal is wonderful, Mrs. Lane," Jay said.

"Kiss ass," I leaned over and whispered to Jay.

"What am I kissing?" He whispered back. Then struggled to stifle a laugh when my cheeks burnt red.

"I will murder you," I whispered.

"You seem pretty worked up, Kitty Cat. Don't want to make everyone suspicious," he whispered. I looked around the table and all eyes were on us. I dropped my eyes to my plate and started shoveling food in as quickly as I could. No one moved or said anything, as I finished my meal, pushed my chair back and brought my plate to the kitchen sink while still chewing my last bite.

I rinsed my plate and put it in the dishwasher before stumbling back upstairs. This trip home literally couldn't get any worse.

Chapter Fifteen

When I got upstairs, I threw off my clothes, pulled on an oversized t-shirt and fell into bed, hoping sleep would numb my mind and provide some relief from my soul searing suffering. But my over thinking brain refused to turn off. I replayed dinner, wondering if everyone could tell that I had kissed Jay. Then I replayed that kiss. That stupid, impulsive, drunken kiss. What the hell was I thinking? Obviously, I wasn't thinking at all, but I would have to live with that choice until I found a way out of here. Or until Jay went back to New York City.

The next morning, I woke up in the dense fog of a hangover, regretting all my life choices.

"That was really dumb," I said to myself as I rolled out of bed. On my nightstand someone put a glass of water with lemon and two Tylenol. Only four people had access to this room and all four of them were just as unlikely culprits of a good deed as the next. But I threw Tylenol back and swigged some water, thankful for my mystery savior. I pulled open my bedroom door before remembering that I was avoiding just about everyone. No one was in the hallway, which was good because I was sure I looked as haggard as I felt. And I was in no condition to interact with anyone. Certainly not in my oversized Rudolph the red nose reindeer tee.

I walked through the hall as quietly as possible, which wasn't quiet at all, when Jay's door opened.

"Oh god please have mercy," I said, pulling at the hem of my shirt while running a hand through my hair.

"How's the hangover?" He asked. I sneered at his perfection. He must have woken up at dawn to shower and get ready for the day, so his perfectly tousled hair looked effortless.

I grumbled in his direction. How had I found myself in the tight hallway with him again?

"That bad?" He asked.

"Why are you talking to me?"

"Should I not be?"

"No, of course not," I said. "Not only did I just wake up, in my own house, which should be a mock free zone, but if we could just pretend the other didn't exist, that would make life so much easier."

"Easier?"

"Oh, my god. What is with the one-word answers?" I asked.

"Make up your mind. First, you don't want me to talk. Now I am not saying enough. Maybe you should figure out what you want Cat Scratch before you start demand things of people."

"I know exactly what I want," I said, closing the gap between us and pointing a finger in his face.

"And what exactly is that?" he grabbed my hand and brought it down forcefully by my side as he used his hulking form to walk me backward across the hall until I couldn't retreat further, and my back was against the far wall. I let out a surprised yip. "Well, Kitty Cat? What do you want?"

Even if I hadn't been completely distracted by his physical presence, I still don't think I would know how to answer. Despite the bravado of my previous answer, it was a complicated question. I'm sure I could have come up with something to say, but not one I was comfortable sharing with Jay. Back in high school, I could have answered easily, now not so much, and I was done being vulnerable with Jay. Jay wanted to intimidate and antagonize me like he always did.

"What I want is none of your business," I said, lifting my chin defiantly. He lifted the hand that wasn't still holding my wrist and clasped my chin.

"Do you want Steve?"

"No," I said. He held me there for several seconds as my head throbbed and my heart thundered. "Are you gonna let me shower?"

He stepped away so abruptly I almost fell and despite my intense hatred, I felt the absence of his body acutely.

When I finally got out of the shower, the house was empty as far as I could tell. I got dressed, made a coffee and walked to the booth, debating if I should tell Jenna that I kissed Jay. My gut instinct told me that I absolutely could not utter those words to another living soul. Jay Crowley has been my enemy for most of my life, and for good reason. His rugged good looks may have momentarily caused a frontal cortex lobotomy during an already vulnerable drunken episode, but he was not the kind of guy I wanted to be with.

For one, hooking up with me would be like some sort of macho bragging rights bullshit. He had never had any feelings for me other than a mix of indifference, disdain, and mocking amusement. I was absolutely positive that I would be another notch in his stupid designer belt that he could laugh about. "Hey bros, can you believe that Cat threw herself at me?" Ugh, the thought renewed my struggle to go on living.

Second, he was not a good person. He had the values of a Wall Street bro mixed with a quarterback who peaked in high school. He only cared about things that provided value in some way for him. There wasn't an altruistic bone in his body. When I was a Girl Scout for half a second at my mother's insistence, he followed me around as I went door to door with my little wagon and stole cookies when I wasn't looking. In the end, I went crying to my mom who made his dad pay for all the eaten boxes, so maybe it turned out alright for me in the end, but still. Who steals Girl Scout cookies?

He wasn't the type of guy I wanted to associate with, and that was final. I pulled open the door to the shop, determined to get the supplies I had intended to get the day before, when I ran head long into my brother, who seemed to be moving at a frantic pace of his own.

"Jesus, Darren, you scared me," I said. Darren stepped back out of the doorway to let me in.

"Nice of you to show up," he said. I shook my head and rolled my eyes.

"Are we ever going to talk about Aubrey?" I asked. I didn't want to be derailed from my purpose of kicking Jay's ass at decorating and sales, but Darren's obnoxious dating life was really bugging me.

"There is nothing to talk about," he said.

"You were making out with my high school bully and Jay's ex long-term girlfriend in the supply closet. I think that might be worth a quick convo," I said.

He took in a long breath before sighing it out, "I knew exactly how you would react to me dating Aubrey, so forgive me for not wanting to deal with your judgmental bullshit right now."

"I think I have a right to be a little judgmental in this case," I said. "She literally tormented me throughout high school. What do you see in her?"

"You don't know anything about me or Aubrey. You have been gone for years and when you are home, everything is about you. You think you aren't judgmental, but you live by these weird standards that you made up and only you know. And anyone who doesn't meet them, you write of entirely," he said.

"I love the top tier deflection happening here."

"I do not have time for this. Can you please just let it go and finish the damn booth?" Darren asked.

"Is everything about making money and being the family

big shot?" I asked. "I'll get the booth done. I don't need this Mr. Bossy-pants vibe you've got going on."

"I am not being bossy. I am being realistic. You are running out of time, and it doesn't seem to matter to you at all," he said. "I know this is just a little holiday distraction for you, but it matters to me."

"Of course, it matters to me."

"Because you need to show up Jay? Yeah, I know. Everything is about you," he said.

"What the fuck? Where is this coming from?" I asked. "I have always put my all into the Christmas booth. Why are you being such a jerk about it?"

"I am just...under a lot of pressure," he said, scrubbing his hands down his face.

"What kind of pressure?" I asked. "I thought everything was going great. You took the store online, and according to Mom and Dad, it's created miraculous growth."

Darren deflated before my eyes with a slump of his shoulders and the dip of his head. "Mom and Dad don't know," he said.

"Don't know what?" I asked. He looked up then, studying my face. "What's up?"

"I need you not to tell them. Unlike the Aubrey thing, this is actually important. I am going to tell them, but only when I have good news to cushion it."

"What is going on? Can you just tell me?"

"The shop isn't doing well."

Chapter Sixteen

"I borrowed too much money, that I haven't been able to pay back," he said. I stared at him with wide eyes, trying to reconcile my amazingly successful brother with this sad, struggling man he described. "I just wanted the store to be something bigger than the holiday shop in a tiny beach town. I borrowed money for the website, marketing, expansion into more products and different markets."

"Why? The shop has always done fine. Was it struggling or something?" I asked. This was a side of my brother I had never seen before.

"Not exactly, but it was really just enough to get by. Mom and Dad deserve to retire, and I worried that they would never have the means to with the shop pulling in the figures it was doing. And..." I could tell he wasn't sure if he wanted to say the next part. "Mom and Dad always put so much pressure on me. They always had this idea that I was some sort of genius, and then I ended up back home, working on the store. I didn't want to disappoint them."

Wow. I blinked several times. I had never thought about the kind of pressure Mom and Dad had put on Darren or its effect on him. I was always too busy feeling sorry for myself. I always just assumed he loved being the favorite. Maybe being the fuck-up had its benefits.

"But do you think the holiday street fair will be enough?" I asked.

"I just want something to show that I am not a total screwup. I want one success even if it is small." His words reflected exactly what I had been feeling, and the revelation that Darren and I had more in common than I thought was strange, to say the least. "Anyway, I know you are pissed about Aubrey and Jay and the store, but Aubrey has been the only person around. She listens and supports me, and I hope, when you are done being mad, you can try to get to know her. I don't think she is the same person she was in high school."

"I'll try," I said.

"I appreciate that," he said. I wasn't sure what to do with myself then. Darren and I weren't big on sibling closeness, so it just felt kind of awkward. I nodded and walked past him to get to the supply closet. At least I knew I wouldn't find him making out with Aubrey this time. Still, I opened the closet carefully, bracing for some new surprise.

When there wasn't one, I gathered the stuff I wanted, packed away carefully in plastic bins. Suddenly, I viewed it with different eyes. The stupid contest between Jay and I didn't matter so much. We had to sell more this season than any past years. I wished I could focus on myself, the paper I was supposed to be writing, my own future, but instead all I could do was worry. Despite Darren's assumption, I cared a lot about the shop and our parents. I finished grabbing what I needed and went back outside.

"What do you mean, Darren?" Mom said. She was using her strained, fake calm voice that she normally only reserved for me. *Oh shit, did she somehow find out about the loans?* I thought.

"It slipped my mind. I thought Jay was managing the booth, and I didn't put the order through," Darren said.

"What's going on?" I asked, dropping my bins in front of the booth where mom stood in her long red wool coat that made her look like Mrs. Claus. Jay stood behind her looking uncharacteristically concerned while Darren looked down-right frantic.

"Your brother didn't order enough of the chocolate for the hot cocoa," mom said. Every year, we gave out free hot cocoa that surpassed every other booth on the street. It was a recipe that my mother and father kept so tight-lipped, even I hadn't been privy to it, but I did know my mom insisted on some fancy chocolate that she bought from a specialty candy shop three towns up the shoreline.

I always thought she did that just to throw people off her scent. All the shop keepers were up in each other's business, which made it extra hard to keep any secrets. Either way, I felt a sudden drop in stomach as if I had reached the top of a rollercoaster and hit the zero-gravity free fall. Maybe it was stupid, but not having our cocoa would be a disaster. Especially if we needed to draw in more shoppers than ever before.

I thought if I ever witnessed my brother fail, I would revel in it. I would be justified and vindicated and blissfully happy all at once. I could laugh and point and rub it in his face. But seeing his misstep now just made my heart hurt. He looked embarrassed and so, so sad.

"I'll go get some. It's not that far. I'll drive up to Ocean Park, get what we need and be back before it is even dark," I said.

"Will it fit in your Prius?" Jay asked.

"Yes, of course. I know my Prius is tiny, but it's not that small," I said.

"I don't know, Cat. I don't want you driving in the snow, and you need to finish the booth," Mom said.

"I can do the booth and get the chocolate," I said. "It will take me twenty minutes to finish the booth. And it isn't snowing."

"It is going to snow," Mom said. We all looked to the sky simultaneously as if it held some weather secret we could immediately discern. Then I came to my senses and pulled out my phone.

"It says eighty percent chance of snow," I said. "I think it will be fine. Besides, what choice do we have? We need that chocolate."

"I'll drive her in the truck," Jay said. I turned to him like he spoke another language.

"That might work," Mom said.

"I don't need a ride," I said.

"I would feel much better if Jay went with you," Darren said.

"That's cool. I wouldn't," I said.

"Don't be so stubborn," Mom said. "We need the chocolate. It's going to snow, and Jay has been generous enough to offer you a ride. It is the perfect solution."

"Why can't Jay go solo? Then I could work on the booth," I said.

"Catherine, you don't have to be so difficult. We aren't going to make Jay travel alone," Mom said.

"Why not?" I said.

"Because he is our guest," she said.

"He seems like less of a guest than I am these days," I said.

"Don't be ridiculous," Mom said.

"Okay mom," I said, trying to head off a lecture. "I guess. I'll get my purse."

Chapter Seventeen

The car rumbled out of the driveway as an uneasy feeling settled in my stomach. *It's fine,* I told myself. I had no choice. I can withstand a few hours in the car with this man. I survived my whole life with him in my general orbit. I could survive this too. We could listen to some music, stare out the window in awkward silence and absolutely not, under any circumstances, talk about the drunken kiss.

I studied the stereo, connected to his phone, trying to figure out how to switch to the radio without turning off GPS. It was much more advanced than my ten-year-old car.

"Ah ha," I said, as I pushed the radio button. The speakers came instantly to life, blasting "White Christmas," loudly enough to shake the speakers. I scrambled to turn the volume down, and of course Jay was laughing when I finally got the music under control.

"You are the only person I know that still listens to the radio," he said.

"I'm not about to look through your phone for music. I'm sure I would be traumatized by what I found," I said.

"Oh yeah? What do you think you would find?"

"I don't know...maybe you keep pictures of all the bodies in the basement." I said.

"I live in a high rise."

"I'm sure you would find a way around that small detail with all your ingenuity."

"Look at you throwing out compliments. If I didn't know you any better, I might think you actually liked me."

"Not a chance."

"Why is that?" He asked. I turned a full 180 degrees in my seat to level a look of disbelief his way.

"I knew you were a jerk, but I didn't realize you were dense too," I said. We had only made it to the outskirts of town, and a stray flurry hit our windshield before melting immediately. That didn't bode well for a quick trip.

"Speaking of jerks," he said. "You aren't exactly nice."

"Why should I be nice to you?"

"Why shouldn't you be? Why do you hate me?"

"I'm not trying to be mean, but do you really lack the critical thinking skills that you don't know? From the moment you became friends with Darren, you have gone out of your way to torment me. When we were young, you played pranks at my expense, you came up with stupid nicknames, you told everyone at school private things that you learned about me from Darren.

"When we got into high school, you recruited your girlfriend to help torture me, you spread rumors, you made the whole football team show up at my art show and make fun of me. You have had a perpetual frown in my presence unless you were laughing at me. You were always just so cool, and you considered everyone outside of your clique as losers. You thought you knew better than everyone. All you do is criticize and judge. No one could possibly live up to your standards." I couldn't seem to stop myself once I got started.

"Even your friends, like Darren, weren't cool enough for you. You found the things that make people feel vulnerable or self-conscious and you exploited them. But the truth is, you aren't cool at all. Underneath that calloused exterior, you are just a boring, cookie-cutter guy who can't do anything but copy trends and shit on things that make everyone else happy, probably because deep down you aren't happy at all. I don't know if you have ever been happy a day in your life."

He was quiet for a while. "Well, don't hold back, Kitty Cat," he said.

"Sorry," I said, sullenly.

"You aren't exactly innocent."

"Seriously? How so?" I asked.

"You are pretty judgmental yourself. You give Darren shit all the time."

"Okay, that doesn't exactly compare to bullying me for my whole life," I said.

"I didn't bully you," he said.

"Hmm," I said. "We will have to agree to disagree." I tuned out and watched through the window as "White

Christmas," changed to, "Joy to the World." We must have been on the easy listening station that switched over to Christmas classics for the months of November and December. Outside the window, the world had that muted pre-snow feeling. We drove the main road along the shoreline with the stretch of beaches on one side and cute, million-dollar bungalows on the other.

Growing up in a vacation destination had its drawbacks, like big crowds four months out of the year, empty streets the rest, and a tiny school where everyone knew each other's business, but whenever I let myself slow down long enough to appreciate it, I recognized how lucky I had it. We existed in a sort of buffered calm that most people only felt on vacation. Sure, there was stress and work, but that all melted away the second my toes hit the sand, or I walked the smooth wood planks of the board walk. That feeling was the essence of my photography back when I let myself enjoy it. Every picture was an opportunity to capture the little bit of magic that infused my life at the beach. I tried to reclaim that sense of peace now as I watched the world pass by, but even the distant ocean wasn't powerful enough to dent the uncomfortable silence I found myself in.

"You aren't wrong," Jay said, then cleared his throat.

"I rarely am," I smirked with a sidelong glance.

"I bet you aren't," he said.

"Wow, now look who is throwing out compliments," I said. "You are a changed man."

"I guess you bring out the best in me," he said. I felt his gaze move in my direction, but I kept my eyes glued out the side window. I certainly didn't want to see the mockery in his eyes, and on the off chance there was something even partially genuine there that would be infinitely worse. I did not want to have any more sympathy for Jay Crowley than I already developed after the Aubrey saga. I wondered if Darren ever talked to Jay about that. Part of me wanted to ask while another part screamed, stay out of it!

I sighed, deciding to get comfortable for the long haul. I pulled my legs up under me, reached into my bag, and pulled out a new crochet cozy project. I probably should have been mulling over my essay outline on my phone, but I could tell I wasn't in the head space to think or plan or write. Not with Jay so close. Although, I wasn't in the right head space more often than not. Alright, fine, I was never in the right head space. I was avoiding my outline and essay like the toxic joy kill that it was. The other people in my final semester all had this feral, compulsory style where they could study, write and work anywhere, sitting in a tree like guerrilla warfare for students, waiting for the bus, or while their best friend talked their ear off.

I could only work if the circumstances were absolutely perfect, and given my mental instability, that meant I rarely did much at all. My fellow wannabe psychologists gave me all kinds of tips and tricks, but nothing ever really worked. I knew there was a life lesson there, but I wasn't ready to analyze yet what it was. And now, I had the benefit of the shop on the brink of disaster to throw myself into.

"Are you...crocheting?" Jay asked with a side-long glance in my direction.

"I like to sell my Christmas cozies in the shop. Besides, what else am I supposed to do? You are't exactly a great conversationalist," I said, feeling instantly stupid in the way only Jay could manage to induce. Jay had a way of belittling me with a simple condescending phrase, which left me feeling like either a stupid child or a complete loser.

"No, it's cool," he said with a laugh in his voice.

"I get it. I'm a nerd. At least I have hobbies. What do you do for fun that is so much cooler?" I asked. I dropped my crochet in my lap and crossed my arms over my chest, feeling the familiar anger with Jay coming back in full force. Since being home, he had seemed different in a way that I couldn't put my finger on, a little nicer maybe, calmer, less laser focused on ruining my life. But maybe it was all in my head because now he was clearly making fun of me. The silence stretched again as the flurries gathered on the edge of the windshield.

"I don't do anything," he said. "For fun. You are right, at least in that. I am boring."

I rolled my eyes. "Of course, you do things for fun."

"No, I really don't," he said, and he sounded so disgusted with himself that I almost believed him.

"You don't watch a football game? Go out clubbing? Create dating profiles to lure in unsuspecting women?"

"You are so strange," he said. "But no. I go out for happy hours with my colleagues in the city out of obligation. I'll watch a football game because it's on, and it will give me something to talk about the next day at work. And I certainly don't have dating profiles."

"Then what do you do? I mean, with all your free time?" I asked.

"I don't have free time," he said. "Or not much of it, anyway. I'm pretty busy with work. Honestly, I try to stay busy most of the time. When I'm not at work, I try to exercise and read, but that's about it." I wasn't sure how to respond. If I let my impulsive brain have control of my mouth, I would say something shitty about how he deserved it, but I didn't know if my life was all that much better just because I had a few hobbies. I barely had any friends at school. I went out with them a few times for happy hour, but always felt like an outsider looking in. I came home wondering if that feeling was all in my head or if they had felt it too, and it came out subtly in their conversations. I wasn't exactly a workaholic like Jay, but I wasn't a social butterfly, either. It meant in this instance; I didn't really have a soap box to stand on and lecture him from. Instead, I felt a teeny tiny little bit of sympathy. It sounded like a lonely existence.

Chapter Eighteen

"**W**hy not try to, I don't know, step out of your comfort zone, try something different?" I asked after a heart beat of silence threatened to end the conversation.

"I guess it's all the things you said about me. I'm arrogant and rigid and judgmental, but mostly I don't know the first thing about what actually makes me happy. I see other people happy, finding joy in shit like knitting a cozy for their coffee," he said taking a hand off the wheel to gesture toward my crochet.

"It's crochet," I corrected quietly because I physically could not resist an opportunity to correct him.

"But I don't know what that thing is for me. I don't know how to find that thing. My whole life was about behaving properly or working hard. My value, according to my parents, came from my contributions. My mom spent my entire childhood traveling. We moved to Cape Shore because my dad thought that would be enough to keep her happy, she loved the beach, but she was always looking for the next big thing. Nothing was ever enough for her, especially me. My dad, threw himself into his work, always physically present but worlds away. He had little tolerance for a child. He only ever paid attention when I got on the honor roll or made captain of the football team. Even then it was to post on social media or try to engage my mother."

"That sucks. I guess that was why you were such a dick?" I asked. He shrugged. "But why not try to do something different now. You don't have to be your father."

"My value was always equated to my productivity, and I don't know how to untether my self-worth from how much money I make or how successful I am. I don't know how to relax and have fun. It probably doesn't make any sense to someone like you," he said.

"Someone like me?" I asked. "What does that even mean?"

"You have made it your life's mission to single-mindedly follow your passions, even if your passions are super nerdy."

"What are you talking about?" I said, despite the voice of self-preservation shouting in my brain to shut up. "I haven't succeeded in a goddamn thing my whole life. I gave up on my passions with the failed scholarship contest. You have some penthouse apartment, enough money to retire tomorrow, and a swanky job that everyone oohs and ahhs about. I haven't done shit. I have failed at almost everything I have tried. I gave up on photography for psychology. When no one was footing the bill for school, because of course my parents didn't see a point in my education unlike Darren's, I had to bust my ass at a full-time job. Somehow, by sheer luck, I managed to make it to my senior year only to lose my way and hit a roadblock completing my final assignment. Now I am here," I spread my arms wide indicating nothing and everything all at once.

"Back in the same old life, doing the same old things, letting my parents and my brother tell me what to do and how to do it. All I ever wanted was to share my vision with the world. For someone to look at my photos and see into my soul and feel that same spark I feel. But I haven't been able to pick up a damn camera for four years." I felt tears burning in the back of my throat, as I swallowed hard to keep the emotions I didn't want to share at bay.

Why the hell was I doing this? Jay didn't give two shits about my sob story. He was one of the many people in my life who always made a point to remind me just how worthless I was. I remember the look on Aubrey's face when she won the photo contest. That smug, condescending expression, like the world owed her. Then she didn't even end up using the scholarship, which absolutely crushed me. And Jay was right there by her side the whole time, congratulating her while I died inside.

"I always liked your photographs," he said, his voice held a sincerity I had never heard before, and I snorted out a laugh. He was a good bullshitter. "Objectively, by the world's standards, I have achieved the pinnacle of success, but it isn't enough. It isn't ever enough. There is no magic moment where everyone you are trying to impress says, 'there it is. You did it. Now you can go enjoy your life.' You just keep busting your ass day in and day out. If there is something that brings you joy. You have to do it. You have to scoff at them the same way you scoff at me. Otherwise, you turn into me. Boring and miserable. But you, Kitty Cat, you are fun. That's why I like being around you."

"What?" I stammered. "You mean I am fun to laugh at? You don't like being around me unless you are making fun of me."

"No, you are funny, smart, and creative. You've just let the world convince you that you aren't," he said, hands on the wheel, eyes straight ahead as if I didn't occupy the seat right next to him. As his voice trailed off, letting Celine Dion's operatic stylings of the "First Noel," fill the silence, the car felt claustrophobic. Like I couldn't spend another second in the cramp space overcrowded with emotions. I had spent my life thinking I knew Jay, knew exactly who he was and what he thought and now here he was giving me the best pep talk of my life.

"I need a bathroom break," I said. He didn't say anything as we drove the next mile and a half to an exit, so he could find a grubby gas station. He pulled off the quiet highway and pulled into the first open station he found. As soon as the truck stopped, I pushed open the door and made a bee line into the bathroom.

Chapter Nineteen

I regretted my choice as soon as I pushed open the heavy, grimy door into the dimly lit bathroom that looked like it hadn't been cleaned in at least a decade. I wanted to take deep breaths and get my head on straight before getting back into the car, but the smell forced me to plug my nose and breathe only through my mouth as I fell apart in a panic.

"What the hell is happening?" I asked my reflection in the scratched, distorted mirror. I couldn't imagine getting back into that car. Shit was getting far too real for my liking. I needed a reality check. Jay was Darren's best friend. He was an asshole, no matter how good of a kisser he was—at least when I was too drunk to know better. He had bullied me my whole life. I don't know why he was suddenly this nice guy telling me exactly what I needed to hear, but I had to find a way to bolster my defenses. I had to get back in the car and get back to hating Jay. This trip home was hard enough without weird, uncomfortable feelings getting in the way. I had to hold on to the world view that Jay was an asshole. I didn't know what it meant if he wasn't. Had he changed? Had I changed? Had I been wrong all along? The idea made my stomach turn, unless, of course, that was the overpowering smell in the bathroom. "You can do this, Cat. Stay strong."

After spending far too long trying to pull myself together, I left the bathroom and let the crisp, fresh, pre-snow air fill my lungs. The scent of the bathroom dissipated. Jay leaned against the car, legs and arms crossed casually, as if he knew exactly how to stand to show off his muscular arms, tapered waist and chiseled jaw line. Holy crap, I had to pull my shit together. I had spent four years avoiding men, and now I couldn't stop thinking about the one that I should be running far, far away from.

"You ready?" He asked.

"I guess," I said.

He lifted a plastic bag covered in the words, thank you. "I got snacks."

"Cool," I said, brushing past him and reaching for the door at the same time he did. I froze and turned to him; my eyebrows scrunched in anger. "Were you trying to open the door for me?"

"Um, is that okay?" He asked.

"No, no, it isn't okay. You need to cut this nice guy shit out. You are not a nice guy. You are not my friend. You do not open doors. We are going to spend the rest of this trip fighting like we always do. You will tell me that I smell, and I will tell you that your face looks stupid, just like we have done our whole lives. We will get the chocolate, get back home, set up our booth, where I will kick your ass, prove I am amazing, rub your face into your own sad pathetic failure and go back to my life knowing that I left you questioning everything you thought you knew about yourself because I so thoroughly put you in your place like you have deserved your whole damn life. Understood." During my tirade, I had crept closer to Jay.

I stopped breathless, only an inch from his body. My skin tingled with our closeness, betraying the promise I just made. He hadn't taken his eyes from my own gaze the entire time I talked to him. Now there was a mix of unflappable intensity and amusement in his eyes.

"Understood," he said, a smile brightening his face, ending our potent staring contest as a thick snowflake landed on my cheek. He lifted his hand, cupped my chin and rubbed his calloused thumb across my face. I swallowed hard as his touch ran through the entire length of my body, leaving me out of breath. My thoughts turned dirty as I thought about what else he might be able to do with those strong fingers, before I shook my head and pulled away to climb into the truck. I slammed the door behind me both so he couldn't close it for me and so he got my point loud and clear.

He walked around the front of the car, and I had to force myself not to watch the way his red and green sweater moved over his body or his tight jeans framed his ass just so. *There is something seriously wrong with me,* I thought with a shake of my head. I just had to remember the way he hid my book bag every morning before school for an entire month. Or how he read my book of poems out loud to Aubrey and Darren. That one hurt. Okay. I could do this.

He climbed into the truck, filling it with his piney scent. I wondered if he wore that specifically during the holidays or if he always smelled that way. He passed me the bag of snacks and started the car. When I peeked inside, I saw a bag of Funyuns and a bag of combos.

"Ooh pretzel and cheddar," I said.

"They used to be your favorite. I wasn't sure if that had changed," he said.

"How would you know what my favorite car snack is?" I asked. He shrugged. I pulled the Funyuns out and threw them at him as he pulled out of the gas station.

"Hey, those plastic corners are sharp. I could have lost an eye, then no one would be getting cocoa this year."

"Eh, it would be worth it. Especially if you had to wear an eye patch the rest of your life," I said. "You know Funyons are gross, anyway. Freeze-dried onions?"

"I just didn't want you to be tempted to kiss me again," he said, glancing at me from the corner of his eye with a smirk.

"You are a top tier jerk. I was drunk, and I think you took advantage," I said.

"Took advantage while you threw yourself at me? I'll have to be more careful," he said.

"Don't worry, it will never ever happen again. It was a momentary lapse in judgement that we will never talk about," I said.

"Of course," he said, as he opened his Funyuns with his teeth and one free hand while the other stayed on the wheel. "Hey, look at us. Fighting so well," he said.

I rolled my eyes as I popped a combo into my mouth. "Did you ever talk to Darren about Aubrey?" I asked.

"Not much," he said. I watched him for signs of his mood darkening, but I didn't see any. Either he was very good at hiding it, or he didn't feel much of anything. I wouldn't be surprised if he felt nothing. Up until this week, I didn't think Jay was capable of normal human feelings.

"How long have they been seeing each other?" I asked.

"He didn't say," he said.

"He told me that she was a friend during tough times, and then it just turned into more, I guess, but I don't know when that happened," I said. "I'm not sure how to feel about it. Aubrey was kind of terrible when we were in school, but Darren claims she changed."

"She hasn't changed," he said. I swirled my head so quickly I almost gave myself whiplash.

"What?" I asked.

"I don't think Aubrey is capable of change. That's all. But I don't want to get involved." As we spoke, the heavy flakes of snow started falling faster. Soon, I couldn't see grass or sand on either side of us as it turned into a blanket of white.

"But you are capable of change?" I asked.

He shrugged and stayed quiet for a while, and I thought he might never answer. "Maybe I haven't changed at all. Like I said, my life revolves around work. It's possible that everyone I work with thinks I'm as big an asshole as you do. I want to be different, but who knows?" I felt the impulse to re-assure him in some way that he seemed nicer, at least on the surface, than he had in all the years since I met him, but that would be breaking the rules I set for the remainder of the car ride.

"Alright, no more serious talk, please. We are supposed to be mortal enemies, remember?"

"Oh right," he said. "But you did start it."

"Start what?"

"The serious conversation. You asked me about Aubrey, again," he said.

"Do you have to win at everything?" I asked.

"I don't have to, but I do," he said. If I had something else to throw, I would have thrown it.

"This snow isn't looking great," I said, as I pulled up my phone to check the weather app. I wondered how many inches they were predicting now. When we left, the app had suggested only one to three inches, which wouldn't be a problem for Jay's truck, but since the gas station, the snow had started coming down heavy. The scenery had been a wintery wonderland of brown grass covering dunes and tan stretches of sand. Now everything was covered in a thick layer of snow, including the road. I hadn't seen a single plow or salt truck. They must have trusted the predictions the same way I had.

"We should be okay. We are only thirty more minutes away," he said.

He spent the next hour white knuckling the steering

wheel while I squinted out the front, trying to determine where the landscape ended, and the road began. Eventually we saw a salt truck-plow combo passing us in the opposite direction, but only five minutes after it cleared the street, the snow covered it again.

Chapter Twenty

By the time we pulled into the small strip mall that held the artisanal specialty candy shop we had been looking for, I felt sweaty and strung out from the stress of driving through what felt like a blizzard.

"We made it," Jay said, looking at me like he hadn't fully believed we would. Even four-wheel drive hadn't kept us from nearly fishtailing off the road a couple of times.

"Good job."

"I know how awful it would be for you to die in a fiery crash with me as the last person you saw."

"Yep, that would have been pretty bad. What would people have said? All the papers would print our names together, they would bag our bodies together. Not the way I want to go out."

"Wow, you are morbid," he said. "I always thought those black clothes of yours were a goth phase or something."

"Nope, my heart is black as coal," I said. "I guess we have to go in." I wasn't looking forward to climbing through the foot of snow between us and the front door.

"I can go in if you want," he said.

"And be the hero? I don't think so."

"What are you talking about? I'm already the hero in this situation. You faced certain death driving through the snow in your Prius," he said. "I'm your knight in shining armor."

I snorted. "I definitely do not need or want a knight, regardless of the armor."

"Of course, you do," he said with that smirk of his that made my blood boil.

"What makes you think you know what I want in a man?"

"I knew about the combos, didn't I? Beside you wouldn't watch those romcoms obsessively if you didn't want to find love one day."

My mouth drew into a thin line. I hated that he knew so much about me, and I had just learned what an asshole his mom was. I hated even more that he was right. I liked to pretend that I didn't need or want anyone, but I did. I desperately wanted someone to fall in love with me like all those romcoms I grew up with, but I was incapable of letting my guard down long enough to let it happen. "Just because I want to find love one day doesn't mean that I need some sort of savior. I can take care of myself just fine," I said.

"Sure you can, Kitty Cat," he said, pushing his door open and letting the cold sweep through the car.

"Asshole," I whispered.

I trudged through the snow to catch up to him in front of the darkened door.

"Shit," I said, pulling on the handle.

"They can't be closed." He put his face up to the window and cupped his hands around his face. "There are people in there."

He banged on the door with a loud, persistent knock. I watched as the guy inside shook his head and mouthed the word, no. Jay knocked again so hard that I thought he might break down the door. This time, the guy inside unlocked the dead bolt, pulled the door open an inch and said, "We're closed. Haven't you seen the snow?"

"Yes, we just drove three hours in it to get some chocolate," he said.

"I knew we had good chocolate, but I didn't think it was that good," he said. *Hardy-har-har,* I thought. He sounded like my dad.

"Listen, we get chocolate from you every year for our special Christmas cocoa. It's kind of important that we have it."

"I already closed the till," he said.

"I'll pay you double," Jay said.

"No," I whispered, yanking on his sleeve. "We cannot afford to pay double."

"It's fine. I'll pay for it myself," he said. "I'm boring, remember? I have nothing else to spend my money on."

"No," I said. "I don't want to owe you like that."

"You won't owe me anything. We just need to get the damn chocolate." While Jay spoke, the guy was already sliding the chain out of the door, opening it wide and motioning for us to come in. I definitely didn't want to owe Jay, but we couldn't show up back home empty-handed, so I begrudgingly followed along as he bought the chocolate and loaded it into the car.

"See, hero," he said after we had gotten back in the car.

"I should slap that smirk right off your face," I said.

"I didn't think you were into that kind of thing, Cat," he said, clutching his chest in mock scandal.

"I'll make an exception for you," I said, my cheeks burning red despite the chill that still lingered in the car.

"You know I can't drive us home through this, right?" While we were inside, the sky seemed to dump another foot of snow.

"You have to," I said. "We have to bring the chocolate back, and we can't stay here."

"We have to find somewhere to stay for the night. By tomorrow the snow will have stopped, and the plows will have gotten the roads cleared," he said, cranking the heat all the way up.

"I definitely don't want to do that."

"That's a real shame for you," he said. "Buckle up. There are a few inns on the Main Street a couple roads away. We'll drive slowly and find some rooms.

"There aren't going to be any rooms. We are two days from Christmas," I said.

"We'll find something."

"I'll check Airbnb to see if there are any places taking last-minute bookings.

All of his attention turned to maneuvering the car safely through the snow, through the cute beach town. It was similar to the one that I called home, but each town that dotted the shore had its own unique feel, which drew loyal tourists who would argue for their favorite beach's superiority until they were blue in the face. It was something I loved about living at the beach, how attached people were to the place that they vacationed.

The streets were empty save for a few families and couples braving the weather to go for walks or play in the snow. Some shops looked open while others had shuttered their doors, losing out on the potential holiday sales to get their staff home safely. Jay parked the car in one of the many spots along the side of Main Street. Under normal circumstances, we would never have found parking. Lucky us.

We walked along the strip of houses, shops and quaint storybook B&Bs, stopping in each place that looked like it was open.

"I feel like goddamn Joseph and Mary searching for a place to sleep," I said after our third rejection as we were stomping through the too high snow that threatened to reach mind calf in the taller drifts. I worried that frozen snot and tears were plastered to my face from the wind, but there was nothing I could do about my looks at that moment. I was sure my normally perfect cat eye liner was smudged to hell, but we had to find a place.

"Woah, language," Jay laughed. How he could make jokes at a time like this was beyond me.

"Very funny," I said. "What do we do if nowhere has a place?"

"Sleep in the truck?" He said with a shrug.

"I'm going to die out here after all."

Chapter Twenty-One

He pushed open the door to a little bed-and-breakfast that had been created out of an old Victorian house. The floorboards underneath the teal green carpet squealed as we walked inside and started to thaw. While it looked like it hadn't been updated in at least forty years, it was cozy. Off to the right of the foyer, there was a great room with oversized armchairs and a big roaring fire. A tree was decorated within an inch of its life and holly, pine garlands and string lights cover the walls.

"This is nice," I said, gravitating toward the fire while Jay headed to the dining area to see if he could find someone. I knew several owners of bed and breakfasts who only showed up for scheduled check ins and to cook breakfast. I was worried that we wouldn't find anyone to give us a key, although it was a good sign that the front door had been unlocked.

I wouldn't mind if it took Jay an hour to find someone

because I was really enjoying the heat from the fire as I stood with my back facing it. We hadn't been out in the snow for a terribly long time, but without the proper winter gear, I was soaking wet and absolutely freezing. If my mother had been here, she would have been yelling at me about my poor planning and stupid decisions. I often wanted to give her the benefit of the doubt that she loved me and just wanted the best, but it was still hard to withstand the constant critique.

"I have good news and bad news," Jay said, startling me out of my thoughts.

"Okay," I said, drawing out the word to let him know that I didn't appreciate the suspense.

"They have space."

"Oh my god, that is amazing."

"But it's only one room."

"Of course, it is."

"It's the honeymoon suite."

"Holy shit!" I said. "We have to keep looking."

"You know that we aren't going to do that," he said. "We are lucky we found this room at all. You can sleep in the bed. I will sleep on the floor. You can pretend I am not there."

"Unlikely," I said.

"Come on, I already got the key."

"Thanks for getting my opinion first."

"Your opinion is clouded by poor judgement."

"There is that condescension that we all know and love."

"I knew you loved me," he said. "Let's go."

"Ugh! Why are you like this!" He disappeared up the stairs and with a heavy sigh, that could have been confused for a grunt, I was left with no choice but to follow. As I walked through the red carpeted hallway, I watched as Jay turned and went up another thin, creaky staircase that, in any other setting, would feel like the setting of a horror movie. Although, given my current circumstance, I didn't think that was terribly far off.

"Ohhh the penthouse," I said as I followed behind Jay. The stairs had, once upon a time, led to an attic, but the room behind the heavy wooden door had been updated into what I could only be described as a cheesy, eighties suite. The space wasn't huge and was made to feel even smaller by the four-post king sized bed, oversized oak dresser, giant fireplace, a small arm chair, and the two-person whirlpool tub.

"A fireplace," I said with enthusiasm. I crossed the room and knelt in front of the giant hearth and started piling logs onto the iron grate.

"Who taught you how to build a fire?" Jay asked, gently shoving me out of the way so he could kneel too.

"I know how to build a fire," I said, shoving him back.

"No, you don't. There isn't enough oxygen flow between those logs," he said, slapping my hand away to rearrange the logs.

"You don't always have to get your way, you know," I said as I used all of my body weight, which wasn't much given my position on my knees, to knock him over. "I'm going to make the fire my way."

He barely moved, so I leaned into him with our shoulders touching and pushed. He laughed, before he leaned backward and I fell face first into his lap, just barely catching myself. He wrapped his hands around my waist, picked me up with my legs kicking, and threw me onto the bed. When I shifted up onto my elbows, prepared to defend my fire making skills, he climbed onto the bed with a knee on either side of my legs and pushed my shoulders flat against the mattress.

"You stay here," he said. I swallowed hard, looking up into his face that had become suddenly dark after the relatively playful banter we had just had. My whole body felt warm with him hovering just above me. My body was a traitor. I wasn't allowed to get all weak in the knees for Jay Crowley no matter how hot his muscles looked in a t-shirt while holding me against the bed. A flush crept up from my stomach, over my chest, and into my cheeks before I found my voice.

"You know, this is the perfect position to kick you in the balls," I said.

He laughed, leaning down even closer, so his lips brushed my ear and his chest pressed against my breasts. "I didn't know you were into that kind of thing, Cat," he whispered.

The world froze and narrowed to the weight of his body, the smell of his cologne, the feel of his lips on my ear, and my pounding heart. I would have sold my soul in that moment for him to shift slightly and kiss me, despite all the promises I made to myself. But he didn't. Instead, he stood abruptly, leaving me out of breath and wanting on the bed as he turned to start the fire.

I couldn't speak. I could only watch him while his back was turned, studying each muscle as it moved beneath his shirt. And I found myself actually wondering if it would be worth putting up with his personality to get him in bed just once. His personality wasn't all that bad in truth. Sometimes he was funny and had proven kind of nice during the car ride. *Oh my God! What is wrong with me?* I silently yelled at myself.

"There, that's how it's done," he said, standing up and gesturing toward the roaring fire. He had opened his mouth and broken the spell.

"I could have done it better," I said.

"Sure," he said, leaning over and patting me on the head. I got up and stood in front of the fire, hoping the bottom of my pants would dry from the walk in the snow. I had already pulled off my shoes and socks, coat and sweater, leaving me in jeans and a cami, but I didn't have high hopes about my pants drying. I couldn't sleep in them, but I also couldn't take them off and walk around in my underwear. I didn't think Jay would ever try something, and just a few minutes ago, I desperately wanted him to, but there was something really embarrassing about sitting around half dressed.

Chapter Twenty-Two

Once I had warmed up enough, my stomach growled. All I had to eat was some combos in the car.

"Is that your stomach?" Jay asked from the armchair that was a little too close for comfort to my spot in front of the fire, but I couldn't exactly tell him to sit on the floor.

"Mind your business," I said with a glare, wrapping my arms around my stomach. Leave it to Jay to mock completely normal bodily noises. And I had just been thinking positive thoughts about him.

"Let's go get something to eat," he said, standing up as if I didn't have a say.

"I am not going back out in the cold."

"Are you going to starve?"

"Do I get to be warm?" I asked.

"Do you enjoy arguing with everything I say, or do you just feel obligated to?" He asked.

"A little of both."

"Well, I'm going to get something to eat. I suggest you come with me, but I can't make you," he said.

"You could offer to bring me food?" I suggested.

"But then I wouldn't get to spend time with you."

"Since when do you want to spend time with me?" I asked.

"Since always," he said. I snorted a laugh.

"You are a good liar. I guess that helps you with your job," I said.

"Maybe."

I begrudgingly put my sweater, coat, and shoes back on, feeling freezing despite the fire. Outside, I shivered inside my coat until we started walking at a fast pace, and the exercise warmed me up slightly. I didn't know the town well enough to know where to go, and I had to imagine Jay didn't either, but we were on the main stretch of shops, restaurants and inns, so hopefully we would find something. Although neither of us were in any condition for a sit down meal at a high-end place, so we had to find something appropriately dumpy.

Ahead, white and colored Christmas lights strung on every lamppost, tree branch and shop reflected off the snow, making a magical sort of glittery effect. It was beautiful and almost made up for us being back out in the cold.

"Should we test out the competition?" Jay asked, pointing to a small, enclosed booth standing against the snow falling around us. It had a sign that read "Coffee by the Beach," and a young woman, bundled in several layers, served various hot drinks to the few people braving the weather.

"The name is a little too on the nose," I said.

"Totally," he said. "I can't believe they do any business at all with a name like that." We approached the booth and ordered two cocoas. They came to us in paper cups with a generous swirl of whipped cream and little chocolate shavings on top.

"Fancy," I said with equal parts admiration and derision before taking a sip.

"Do you think they use chocolate from the same place we do?" Jay took his own tentative sip and then smacked his lips thoughtfully, as if he were a sommelier tasting some new wine.

"If they are smart, they do," I said, taking a sip. It was rich and sweat and delicious. If it hadn't been so hot, I would have gulped the whole thing down in one long swig. "It's good."

"Really good," Jay said, "although not as good as your mom's."

"They must not know her secret ingredient," I said.

"Love?" He asked.

"An unhinged need to win," I said.

"Aww, just like you. How cute," he said, ruffling my wet hair. I nudged him with my elbow. I had to find a way to get him to stop doing that.

"Oh look. More competition," he pointed to the Christmas shop on the corner. I definitely didn't want to go in there. Sometimes, sussing out the competition was helpful, other times it just made you feel defeated before you got started. Like my essay, that I definitely didn't want to think about. But Jay was already walking in that direction with his long strides without any concern for my shorter legs or lack of proper footwear. Luckily, the overhang from the shops protected the sidewalk to some extent. The paved sidewalk, I noted with a smug superiority. No cobblestone here.

Inside felt marvelous as the warmth thawed my face. My appreciation was short-lived when I looked around. It was the shop of Jay's dreams. No clutter, no tchotchkes, no tacky over the top displays. Everything highly curated and in its place.

"Well, you must be in heaven," I said quietly, feeling the need to whisper like at a museum. This store had not been designed to touch or feel, it had been designed to herd shoppers through aisles to the cash register, purchases in hand. Maybe, in that regard, it was better than our store.

It was too late; the self-doubt came crashing down. I thought about my design for my table in the booth and how silly it probably was. I had settled on nostalgia. I had pulled out bins from Christmas's well passed, with items that meant something to me, and represented a unique moment in time, bubble lights, tinsel, brightly colored garlands, a dancing Santa, all things that reminded me of my childhood, and some things that would remind my parents of theirs. To Jay and the people that set up this store, it would look cluttered and not aesthetic. To me, it felt magical, but maybe that didn't matter.

I blinked hard. Why did I care so much about the booth?

Or my parent's store? I had spent the last four years desperate to get away. Now, I was practically crying at the thought of someone doing it better than me. I had to pull myself together. It didn't matter if I did a shitty job on the booth. It didn't matter if Jay "beat" me. I wanted Darren to succeed, but even that wasn't really my problem, right? I took a deep breath after my little pep talk and saw Jay watching me.

"What?"

"It's not so great," he said.

"Oh please, this is everything you want in a Christmas shop," I said.

"Your shop will always be my favorite," he said.

"It's not my shop."

"Uh oh, don't look now, Kitty Cat," Jay said in an outraged voice. A million thoughts flew through my head. Was Aubrey somehow there, making out with someone else? I couldn't come up with anything else that might scandalize me. "They copied you." When I turned to see what he pointed to, I couldn't help but laugh just a little. It was a basket full of knitted cozies.

I slapped my hand to my chest. "I'm gonna sue. Get me the best big shot, New York lawyer you know."

"I'll call him right away. I'm sure he will move this to the top of his case load," Jay said. I noticed in that moment that we were both smiling like idiots. What the hell was happening to me? Jay had cheered me up? Did we slip into an alternate dimension?

"This place sucks. Let's go." He took me by the hand and pulled me out of the store back into the storm. I could just barely hear "Silent Night" playing across the street, where a band was set up underneath a pavilion with several heaters and open fires surrounded by a plastic enclosure. Little kids ran around and roasted marshmallows while the adults tried to stay warm. Without letting go of my hand, Jay pulled me across the snow-covered street where no cars were driving. It was significantly warmer inside the enclosure, and I felt almost like I was inside of a snow globe. Twinkling Christmas lights hung from the ceiling. The music warmed my soul. Children laughed as they played, and I felt like I could have lived in that feeling forever.

I didn't even notice that Jay still held my hand until he pulled me again, deeper into the tent, closer to the band. By the time I realized what he was doing, it was too late. He put my hand on his shoulder, then wrapped a hand around my waist and started guiding me around the dance floor where two older couples moved around expertly.

"What are you doing?" I asked.

"Dancing." He pulled me closer, so the front of my body pressed up against his and despite the thick coats and cold weather, my whole body felt warm.

"Why?" I asked.

"I am trying to be more like you. Spontaneous. In the moment."

I opened my mouth to argue, but in truth, I didn't want him to stop. It was the most fun I had in as long as I could remember. All we were doing was shuffling around the dance floor, but it was so strange and unusual that it crossed the line into memorable and unique. I didn't care that he was Jay

Crowley, high school bully. I just cared that I was there, listening to the brass band play "Silent Night" in that little tent, surrounded by life and joy. I rested my head on his chest, feeling the rhythm of his heartbeat as we glided over the floor. It occurred to me that I had never done anything like this before and although the rest of my life may have been a shit show, this one moment was kind of a highlight.

When the song stopped, my heart dipped just a little bit. "Thanks," I said, looking up at Jay. "That was really nice."

"Thank you for not murdering me in front of all these people," he said.

"I wouldn't even think about murdering you in front of all these people. Of course, I would do it privately."

"That's a relief," he said. "Let's get you food."

We found a food truck just outside of the pavilion and ordered some hybrid taco, sub sandwich combo that could have only come from the culinary genius of a kitchen on wheels. I ate with abandon as the grease dripped from my fingers and down my lips. I probably ate it in five minutes flat.

"Remember when your mom told you that no boy would ever date you if you ate like that?" Jay asked with a snorting laugh.

"The real question is, why do you remember that?" I asked. I did remember it. Even at the time, I had told her I didn't care if no man ever liked me, but it had been a lie. I cared so much, and it hurt to know she didn't think I would ever be worthy of the kind of love I wanted.

"I thought it was funny," he said.

"Of course, you did."

"I thought your mom didn't know what she was talking about because the way you ate was cute." I had no idea how to respond to that. Of course, that didn't stop my brain from milling over what the hell he meant. Was he just saying that to be nice? Was he joking? Why would he think me eating like a slob was cute? Truly, nothing made sense anymore, but at least we could go back to the hotel and warm up.

Chapter Twenty-Three

The warm glow of the bed-and-breakfast beckoned me as we made our way back through the snow, which still fell steadily, piling up around us.

Inside, I felt bad tracking snow through the lobby and up the stairs, but I didn't have much of a choice. I couldn't wait to cuddle into the warm bed. Until I remembered we only had one. Part of me, some tiny little part, wouldn't have minded Jay's strong arms around me, like they had been when we danced, but my logical brain knew that would end in something terrible.

In the room, Jay stoked the fire while I pulled off my boots, coat, and sweater. I really wanted to take off my wet pants. Eventually, I would have to, but I couldn't bring myself to walk around in panties around Jay. He probably wouldn't even bother glancing in my direction, though.

Once the fire roared and the room was warm and cozy,

Jay grabbed a pillow from the bed and tossed it onto the floor.

"You're going to sleep on the floor with only a pillow?" I asked.

"I don't have any other choices. Besides, the fire will keep me warm," he said. I started pulling open drawers and the small cabinets in the bathroom, looking for an extra blanket.

"Call down to the front," I said.

"This isn't a hotel, Cat Scratch. It's a bed-and-breakfast. The owner was going home when I caught up with him to ask for this room."

There was a long pause as Jay lied on the floor with his arms behind his back.

"We aren't children. I'm sure we can share a bed, so long as you stay on your side," I said. I couldn't believe I was saying it, but it was ridiculous to think that he was sleeping on the hard floor without even a blanket.

"You are the only one who has ever made a move, you know," he said.

"I guess you really want to sleep on the floor," I said, folding my arms across my chest. He sat up and held up his hands innocently.

"Alright, I'm sorry. I would appreciate sleeping in the bed, but only if you are comfortable with it," he said. I wasn't. Or maybe I was comfortable, a little too comfortable.

"It's fine. But turn around, I have to take off these wet pants. I don't want you to see," I said.

"Wow, Kitty Cat, I really didn't know you had it in you," he said with a laugh. I grabbed a throw pillow off the armchair and threw it at his face. "Okay, Okay, I won't look."

He turned to face the far wall as I pulled off my pants as quickly as I could, leaving them in a heap by the fire before I practically sprinted for the bed and pulled up the covers. I felt my face burning, even though I knew he hadn't seen anything.

"You can turn around," I said. He turned and saw me in bed with the covers up to my chin. I started creating a wall of pillows down the middle of the bed.

"I thought you said we weren't children?" He asked as he crossed to the fire, picked up my pants, folded them neatly and hung them on the armchair, angling it so the fire could dry them.

"Everything has to be just so. You couldn't live with my pants in a pile on the floor. What if I wanted them where I left them?" I asked.

"I thought you would want a dry pair of pants, but if you want them in a heap on the floor, I can make that happen," he said.

My eyebrows furrowed, and I let out an inaudible grumble. He was so impossible. It made me nuts that he always had to be right, but it made me even more crazy that he so often was.

"That's what I thought," he said. I lied down in bed, turning away from where he would be sleeping and pulled the covers all the way up. He turned off the light. Then, after a moment of him moving through the dark room, I felt his weight compress the other side of the mattress.

"Goodnight, Cat," he whispered into the mostly dark room, lit only by stray moonlight coming through the cracks in the curtain and the glowing orange of the fire. All things considered, it was very cozy.

I was acutely aware of every inch of my body as the sheets touched my skin, and shifted ever so slightly with the tiny movements he made. The king bed felt incredibly small, as if he were only an inch away from me. I worried if I moved at all, I would find myself pressed up against him. I thought about how he slept. Was he on his back? His side? Was he facing me or facing away? I couldn't turn off my brain.

Then I wondered what he was thinking. What if he hated sharing a bed with me? What if he was already asleep? What if, worst of all, he was thinking about my half naked body separated by only pillows?

"I can feel you over-thinking, Cat," his voice rumbled into the silent room, and I nearly gasped at the sound of it.

"What are you talking about?"

"You are so tense, you are practically vibrating with all the crazy thoughts in your head," he said.

"Me? Crazy? You are the crazy one," I said. *Why am I so lame?* I thought.

"You definitely have a tendency to over-think," he said. "I'm sure that is why you haven't finished your essay yet."

"Way to hit below the belt, as I am just trying to fall asleep," I said.

"I just think you have all these great ideas in your head, and you let your fears get in the way," he said.

I rolled over and propped myself onto an elbow. "Oh

really? And what exactly are you doing by staying in the city, working a miserable job when you actually want to be crocheting coffee cozies instead?"

His laugh vibrated through the bed. "I never said I want to quit my high-paying job to make coffee cozies."

"Close enough. You are over-thinking and worrying about other people's opinion. Who would you be if you weren't some high paid, big shot, city boy?"

"I guess you are right. Maybe you could teach me how to crotchet. Then all my problems would be solved," he said. There was something terribly intimate whispering secrets into the dark with Jay.

"Here is the secret to life, Jay. Everything can be solved with a cozy fire, a walk on the beach, a good book, Christmas lights, and a fun little project. Maybe a cat for good measure," I said.

"Well, at least I have a cat," he said. My whole body went warm as his low voice reached through every inch of me.

"You do not have me," I said.

"Then I guess I am out of luck," the genuine disappointment in his voice left me feeling vulnerable and confused.

"I guess so. Goodnight, Jay," I said, turning back over, closing my eyes and ignoring the feel of his attention still locked on me from behind. Eventually, the bed shifted again as he got comfortable, and my brain settled enough to sleep.

Chapter Twenty-Four

I was vaguely aware of being wrapped tightly in warmth from a firm shape behind me. The room remained blanketed in dark as the minimal moonlight peaked through the curtains and the red glow of dying embers flickered on the ceiling. I squirmed just a little closer against the warmth behind me. I had been having the best dream when a large hand squeezed around my hip before gliding up to my waist, I remembered where I was and who I was with. My eyes shot open. *Shit.*

"Cat," Jay groaned quietly into my ear. His hot breath brushing against my neck and sending electricity racing across my skin. My name on his lips held an unasked question, dripping with need that turned my insides liquid. I knew that my heart thundered so hard, he must have felt it from behind my rib cage.

I couldn't move or think. His hand had frozen an inch away from my breast and I felt the firm, excited length of him pressing against my ass. I tried to move away in the hopes that my brain might start working again, but before I could get more than an inch, Jay grabbed my hip and rolled me hard onto my back before climbing on top of me. I couldn't breathe. There was just enough light to see the intensity on his face an inch above me. Then my mind turned entirely to mush as he lowered his hips between my legs. I could feel his thick, hard cock pressed tightly against my panties. I was very aware that there were only two thin pieces of fabric keeping us apart.

A gasp escaped my lips as my hips started grinding against his erection without my permission, rubbing myself along his length as a growing warmth developing between my legs. He wrapped his hands around my hips, his fingers digging into my ass as he held me down to keep me from moving.

"Cat," he growled again. "What are you doing?"

"I don't know," my voice came out breathy. I had no idea what the hell I was doing. My body was on fire with need in a way I had never felt before. In the past, every guy I had ever dated started out as either a passionate, but ill-informed crush or someone who was just really persistent, and any intimacy felt kind of like a chore. Maybe my anger, dislike, and all the tension that I carried for Jay turned these moments of physical tension into a bonfire of lust. It didn't make any sense, but with Jay on top of me, nothing did. I should have been pushing him off me, or telling him to sleep on the floor, but I couldn't.

I could still feel his hard cock just barely touching me.

My hips wrestled against his hands as I closed my eyes and bit my lip, desperate for the sensation of his full weight again.

"What do you want, Cat?" He had moved from whispering in my ear to let his lips graze lightly along my neck, sending shivers over my body as the length of his chest pressed down on top of me. Still, his hips hovered just barely out of reach. I didn't know how to answer that question without sounding pathetic. I couldn't possibly admit how badly I wanted him, although surely he could already tell.

"Do you want me to touch you Cat?" He asked. "Do you want me to run my hand along your bare skin, up under your flimsy little tank top to cup your breast or rub my thumb along your nipple?"As he spoke his hand slid up from my hip, to my waist, to my ribs, bunching my shirt up as his hand touched bare skin stopping just short of my breast. I could feel his thumb inching just slightly upward, and I couldn't breathe. All I could do was feel. "Do you want me to slide my fingers underneath your panties? Find your opening and slide inside?" Again, as he spoke, I felt his other hand move from my hip as his thumb slid under the edge of panties. I nearly screamed out, but he didn't touch me. His fingers stayed just out of reach. "Do you want me to push my hard cock inside of you and fuck you so hard you come for me?"

"Oh God," I let out a whimper. "Please."

"Please what, Cat?" He asked. He pressed a light kiss to my neck, moving from my jaw line down, excruciatingly slowly. "What do you want, Cat?" Was he really going to make me say it? He was awful. "You are overthinking,

Cat." He said, lifting further off me to look me in the eye. I let out a huff in frustration. "Just say it. Say what you want."

"Fine. I want you," I said, making it clear that I wasn't the least bit happy about this revelation. He lowered himself back down so the weight of him trapped me against the mattress. Once again, I felt his firm erection between my thighs and couldn't stop the sigh escaping my lips. I squirmed my hips around, feeling the exquisite sensation of him. But when he pressed his lips to mine, my thoughts vanished, and I was lost in the kiss. He used his tongue to part my lips as I became completely pliable to his will. His tongue brushed against mine, and I felt the power there, that I would have liked to feel other, lower places.

As he kissed me, he moved his hand along my bare skin, slowly, lightly until he reached my breast. I let out a gasp as he cupped my breast in his large palm and let his thumb play over my hard nipple. He moved his lips from my mouth back to my jaw line, down to my collar bone, before pulling down my tank top and darting his tongue over my nipple. I moaned.

"Do you like that?" He asked. I was angry that he had stopped.

"Yes," I said quickly in the hopes that he would keep going. As he lowered his mouth back to my breast, I felt his thumb slide further into my panties until he reached my opening. His thumb glided with the lightest pressure over my wet, aching pussy, sending shivers radiating through my body.

"Oh God, you are so wet," he mumbled, which only made me more excited.

"Please," I moaned. I had to feel his fingers on me, in me.

"Please what?" He asked, fingers hovering under my panties, just out of reach.

"Please, please touch me," I said, feeling my cheeks burn red. But a heartbeat later, he slid a finger inside of me and I moaned, arching my back. He moved his finger in slow motion, in and out of me until I thought I might explode with need. When he slid a second finger in, it felt full and tight as he finger fucked me, pumping in and out, faster and faster before his thumb found my clit, rubbing with gentle pressure. It only took a few seconds before the warmth that had built between my legs rushed through as my orgasm shook my whole body.

When my orgasm faded and my brain started functioning again, I realized that I was in bed, mostly naked, with Jay on top of me. He had a primal look of want on his face as he stared at me. Suddenly, I was nervous and self-conscious. I didn't know what to do with myself. He had taken care of me, so I imagined it was only fair that I took care of him. I let my hand glide down the front of his bared chest, feeling every inch of his firm muscles. I reached under his waist band and wrapped my fingers around his large, smooth cock. His breath caught as I slid my palm up and down the length of him, slowly, watching his intense expression.

As I pumped his cock faster and faster, he closed his eyes and groaned before grabbing my hand and pulling it away. I wasn't sure what I had done wrong. I thought that was what he wanted.

"No," he said, pinning my hand to the bed as his hard cock pulsed with unmet need. I looked at him with wide, unsure eyes before he bent forward and kissed me again, his cock settling between my thighs and making me wet all over again. "I want to take my time with you." His voice reached through me as if he had touched every inch of my skin. He started by pulling my tank top up over my head. I sat up slightly to help him slide it off, before falling back against the bed. My full breasts exposed, nipples hard.

I didn't know what to expect, but he started at my lips before moving to jaw, then my neck. He ran his mouth across my collar bone and dipped down to my breast. He cupped them before squeezing hard and teasing at my nipples with his tongue before letting his mouth trail down my stomach and onto my hip bone. By the time he kissed my thigh, I was squirming with anticipation.

He looped his fingers around my panties and slowly pulled them down, kissing the inside of my thighs as he went. Once my panties were off, he moved my knees apart. I should have felt self-conscious. I always had in the past, but I couldn't think past my need as he moved his face between my thighs. He parted my pussy with his fingers before darting his tongue inside and licking forcefully along my clit. I squirmed and moaned as he found his rhythm, exploring me with his lips, tongue, and fingers. I felt each movement deep in my stomach as the sensations started spreading through my body. I tilted my head back and ran my fingers through his hair, pushing him harder against me.

He stopped just before the orgasm tore through my body, and I let out a moan of frustration, yanking at his hair and pushing him between my legs. But it was no use. He sat up easily, staring down at me. The room was dark, but the moonlight played across his body, highlighting ever curve and shadow of his broad chest and rounded muscles. His cock was impossibly big pulsing with need out of his boxer briefs, and I worried for a split second it would't fit.

"What do you want, Cat?" he asked me again, and I wasn't sure if I would be able to form a coherent thought.

"Oh God. I want you," I said. He watched me for a heartbeat, and I was worried that he wasn't going to continue. His stare was so intense, and I had no idea what he was thinking.

"You really want this, Cat?" He asked again with sincerity. At first, I thought he had been teasing me, forcing me to say something that was embarrassing. But now, I couldn't tell. I thought maybe he really wanted to be sure that I wanted this. Wanted him. But there was no doubt in my mind that there was nothing I wanted more in the world. Tomorrow, I may feel differently, but that was future Cat's problem. Present Cat needed Jay like I had never needed anything in my life.

"Yes," I said.

"I am going to fuck you now, Cat," he said with such confidence that I let out a little whimper. As soon as he said it, he pulled his boxer briefs off, exposing the full thick length of himself for me to admire. He leaned down again, propping himself over me on his elbows. He kissed me long and hard. Then he pressed his thick, ridged cock against my wet opening, pulling a gasp from my lips. He pushed himself inside of me slowly until I didn't think I could take anymore. I was tight and wet around him as eased himself inside.

"Oh god you're tight," he moaned as I felt his cock move slowly out of me.

"No," I whispered before he pressed himself back inside of me, filling me all the way with his huge, impossibly hard cock. I had never felt anything like it before. Soon, he started moving his hips up and down. Pushing in deep and hard as the sensations built. I watched his muscles tighten above me as his own pleasure built, the faster he moved.

"Oh God, I have wanted this for so long," he groaned. For a second that gave me pause, and I thought about asking what the hell he meant, but then he reached his hands under my ass and lifted my butt halfway off the bed, so he could thrust harder and deeper. He pushed into me harder and faster with such passion that the headboard knocked against the wall, his hands squeezing, muscles bulging under the effort not to come right away. I watched him on top of me move with uninhibited passion, and lust, and a new orgasm rushed over me like a tumultuous wave on the ocean, making my body burn and my brain go fuzzy. Above me, Jay came hard and fast with a loud moan as every muscle in his body tensed with buildup and release.

Chapter Twenty-Five

I woke up the next morning to my phone vibrating against the nightstand. It took me a minute to remember where I was. As soon as I did, a rush of feelings threatened to overwhelm me. *Holy shit, I slept with Jay. Holy shit. Holy shit. Holy shit.* I thought, bringing my hands to cover my face.

The sun trickled through the cracks in the heavy drapes, but I couldn't tell how late I slept. It could have been six in the morning or noon for all I knew.

The shock, embarrassment, confusion, and just a teeny tiny bit of excitement that flashed before my eyes amplified when I saw Darren's name on my caller ID. I froze in panic and indecision until the call went to voicemail, and I could breathe just a little bit again. I turned carefully, moving as little as possible because I wasn't ready to face Jay. I couldn't even begin to process what the hell happened or how I felt about it. Behind me, Jay slept with his lips slightly parted, his chest lifting with heavy rhythmic breathing.

Thank God, I thought, *he's still asleep.* I needed all the time I could get to wrap my head around the terrible decisions that were made last night. How the hell had I let my judgement slip so egregiously? Here's what I knew.

One: last night, I slept with Jay.

Two: it can never happen again.

Three: Darren can never know for reasons that alluded me at the moment, but I was sure would become crystal clear the second he found out.

Four: Jenna probably shouldn't know either, although I hated keeping shit from her, and I would probably cave, anyway.

Five: At some point Jay would wake up, and I would have to talk to him. Maybe I should Uber a ride home?

I was too busy making a stupid list in my head to notice Jay's movement beside me. When I did, it was too late. He lay there, eyes open, looking at me.

"Stop over-thinking," he said.

"Easy for you to say," I said. "I am sure you do this all the time. But I don't. Oh, my God." I lifted my hands to my face again. "Can we just not talk about it?" Then my phone buzzed. My head swiveled so fast, I could have given the girl from The Exorcist a run for her money. "It's Darren," I whispered, as if Darren could hear me through the phone. "He cannot know."

"Answer it," he said. "He's probably worried."

"No, I am not ready. I haven't prepared a lie."

"A lie for what?" He asked, propping himself up, revealing his bare chest. *Holy shit, was he still naked?* That's when I looked down and realized I too was still naked. I yipped and pulled up the blanket, covering my breasts. Jay let out a little laugh and I wasn't sure if I wanted to cry or punch him or both.

"For this," I said, gesturing between us.

"I don't think he knows about this yet," he said.

"No, not yet. Not ever," I said. "Oh God, this is just going to be another thing that you hold over my head and use against me, isn't it?"

"I have no idea what you are talking about. But as far as Darren and anyone else knows, we drove out to get the chocolate and got snowed in," he said.

"Right, that's right," I said.

"No one has to know until you are ready," he said. Maybe it was meant to be strangely comforting, but there would never be a time that I was ready.

"Alright, we have to go."

"You have to call Darren."

"You call him. Tell him I'm asleep. No wait, you will tell him the truth. No, you aren't allowed to talk to Darren ever again," I said.

"He is my best friend. I am going to talk to him again," he said.

"Not anymore, he isn't." I said. "I'm calling him back, and then we are going. Turn around so I can get out of bed."

He lifted his eyebrows with a smirk but turned around without argument. I stood up and found my tank on the floor, grabbed my pants and hurried into the bathroom, where I showered. It was probably the fastest shower of my life because I just wanted to get the hell out of there. I threw on my day-old clothes, tossed my hair into a bun and walked out with my phone already to my ear. Darren had called and texted five more times since the last time I checked. I passed through the room, went to the door, so I didn't have to watch Jay look out the window with his shirt off like we had all the time in the world.

"Get dressed," I mouthed on my way out. I walked down the rickety stairs before winding down to the main floor to find a quiet corner near the fire to talk.

"Cat?" Darren said. As soon as he answered, I felt bad. He sounded so worried. "Where have you been? Did you get the chocolate?"

Alright, maybe I could feel less guilty since it sounded like he only cared about the chocolate. "Don't worry, I am fine, Darren. Thanks for asking," I said.

"I figured you were since you finally called," he said.

"Yes, we got the chocolate. We got stuck here in the snow, but we are heading back now."

"Will the booth be ready?" He asked.

I sighed. I guess I couldn't blame him for being stressed. A lot was riding on the next day's worth of sales. "Yes," I said. "I'll see you soon."

"Alright, hurry home," he said.

"Will do." I hung up the phone, angry that I had somehow let myself get dragged back to being in Darren's shadow. I wanted to help him succeed. I didn't wish for my brother to fail, but I just wished that my whole Christmas break had turned into helping him and my parents, which had led, inadvertently, to the insane situation I found myself in with the man waiting for me upstairs.

Admittedly, it wasn't directly their fault that I had no self-control last night, but I think they should take some of the blame, at least. "When I get back, I'll finish the booth, then lock myself in my room and write my paper," I promised myself, as the familiar anxiety rose in my gut at the thought of finishing my essay. I could never pinpoint exactly what caused the fear. Was it worry that I couldn't do it? Fear that it just wouldn't be good enough? Or was it something else? Something else I didn't think I could face at that moment, like some sense that this wasn't the exact right path for me? Even if it wasn't, there was nothing I could do about it. There was no other direction to go.

"Enough procrastinating," I said out loud before turning and heading back to the room. Inside, Jay had made the bed and had left out a steaming mug of coffee with my name written on a scrap of paper underneath it. He made the bed... in a B&B...wow. The coffee smelled amazing. He must have gotten it from the kitchen while I was on with Darren. The steamy liquid in my mug was a light brown, the right color. I took a sip. It was perfectly sweet. How the hell did Jay know how I liked my coffee? Was he really some creepy stalker this whole time? Once again, I remembered what he said last night and my whole body went warm as I sat in the armchair, my legs tucked up under me.

When Jay came out of the shower, that was where he found me, still sitting, pondering the previous night.

"Finally," I said, because I couldn't say anything nice. "Let's go."

"What did Darren have to say?" He asked as I walked out the door and down the stairs.

"He wanted to know if his chocolate was okay," I said.

"You know he is just worried," he said.

"I get it, but I don't have to like it," I said. Jay checked out, settling the bill, I imagined. I would have to pay him back at some point. I definitely didn't want to owe him again.

"How much was it?" I asked when he joined me in the truck.

"Don't worry about it," he said.

"But I will worry about it."

"Of course you will. But I'm not telling you how much because I won't enable your anxiety."

"I'll find out somehow," I said. He pulled out of the parking lot and started toward the highway. The anxiety that had begun with the thought of finishing my essay only grew with the silence in the car. I couldn't decide if my week at home was turning out as bad as I thought, or worse. Then Jay shifted in his seat, and I saw his fingers flex around the steering wheel, pulling the muscles in his forearm tight, sending warmth burning through my body, and I decided it was worse. Definitely worse. How could I have let this happen?

"Our drive back should be shorter," he said. "We should be home in an hour."

"Great," I said. Jay was silent as he flipped on the radio.

"Did I convert you?" I asked.

"Look at me, living on the edge. Letting the radio decide what we listen to," he said.

"You are a new man," I said.

"Guess all it took was a cat," he said with a side glance and a smirk. I closed my eyes and willed a patch of black ice to take me out.

"You are..." I began.

"Funny? Charming? Great in bed?"

"Arrogant? Stupid?"

"Handsome? Dashing?"

"Selfish? Oblivious?" I said.

He shrugged, "I'll take it so long as you agree with my adjectives, too."

"I plead the fifth," I said. The smooth voice of the easy listening channel came on and announced their love of all things Christmas before introducing Kelly Clarkson's "Underneath the Tree," which always managed to give me the big time Christmas feels. Jay had been right; I was a romantic at heart. I had no idea how I had such bad luck in that department, and somehow, I had ended up here with Jay in this terrible, awkward, sort of, maybe, interesting situation. *Holy shit, what if this was my romantic moment like in all the movies?* I looked at Jay with wide eyes, trying to really see him. Could this actually be something? That would require him liking me as more than a one-night stand though, which I didn't think was possible for him. I doubted he was capable of real romantic feelings. Look at how he felt about Aubrey. And they had dated for years.

"So, what's your essay about?" He asked.

"Ugh," I groaned. "A whole lot of nothing. It's supposed to be a synthesis of my entire college career, but as of now, it's about how well I can bullshit."

"Sounds great," he said.

I glared at him.

"How's New York?" I asked.

"Ugh," he groaned, mimicking me with a smirk.

"Seriously?"

"I miss the beach every time I am away," he said.

"That is surprising," I said.

"Why?"

"Because you left and never came back."

"I come back every chance I get, but without my parents here, I only have friends to come back to, and I lost touch with everyone but Darren. I love it here. It is slow and quiet and stress free."

"That is what vacation always feels like," I said, thinking of the tourist mindset that crowded in during the summer.

"Maybe, but New York City is busy and loud and easy to get lost in, both literally and metaphorically. You could walk for blocks and not see a single familiar face. You could live there for years and go days without seeing the same person twice," he said.

"Sounds kind of amazing. Maybe we could ditch Darren

and the booth and run away to the city, to blend in with the crowd and become street performers."

"I'll take you anywhere you want to go, Cat," he said. In the quiet insulation of the car, buffered away from real life, I was inclined to believe him. But we had to go back, and we both knew it. At least one of us was looking forward to it.

Chapter Twenty-Six

We pulled into the lot behind the store and the anxiety that had dissipated from spending the car ride alone with Jay came back in full force. I turned to him, grabbed his sweater, pulled him close to me over the center console, so he knew I was serious.

"No one can know," I said, locking eyes with him. His gaze strayed from my eyes to my lips, and I felt lightheaded as desire mixed with my worry.

"Okay," he said without any of his usual ribbing, which I could have kissed him for, except I couldn't possibly do that, of course.

"Okay." I let him go and smoothed out his sweater, feeling the tight muscles hidden beneath it, remembering what his bare skin felt like pressed hard against my body last night. "I guess we have to do this."

"Yep," he said, pushing open the car door, grabbing some chocolate and walking toward the booth.

"Jesus Christ, I didn't think you guys would make it," Darren said.

"I told you we would," to my great chagrin, Aubrey stood leaning against the booth, looking at the closed bins and partially decorated space with her usual disdain that gave me war zone flashbacks to high school, which made me want to put distance between Jay and me. He had been pretty cool during our little excursion and scorching hot at the same time, Jesus when did I get so cheesy, but now that we were back in real life, staring down the booth, Darren, Aubrey, my parents and the Christmas party, my growing feelings were significantly dampened.

"We gotta finish," Darren said with a frantic voice.

"I'll get the hot plate and the cocoa urn," Jay said. It was really a coffee urn, but we repurposed it for our specialty cocoa.

"I'll finishing setting up. It will only take me thirty minutes," I said. I felt Aubrey's eyes on me as I brushed past her into the booth. I thought Darren had some nerve rubbing her in our faces after we had braved a blizzard for him. I knew that he wanted me to give her another chance, but I wasn't in the mood. Maybe Jay had grown up, or I had somehow grossly miscalculated who he had been when we were younger, but I didn't have the patience to deal with Aubrey.

As I opened the bins that I had been planning on using, I flashed back to the Christmas shop Jay and I had visited the night before. I tried to keep my mind from remembering the rest of the night, although I didn't really want to sit with the memory of the Christmas store, either. My booths had always done well. I had always had some spark of creativity that managed to bring people in and lead them to buy things, so this year shouldn't have been any different, but somewhere along the path of growing up, being on my own, and facing failures, that spark had faded. Sometimes it felt hard to access at all, clouded by doubt and overthinking.

There was nothing to be done about it, though. The booth had to get done, whether the creativity flowed or not. I took a deep breath and tried to tune out Aubrey's hovering. When I turned around in the process of unpacking and choosing products to sell and decorations to use, I saw that Darren had left as well, leaving Aubrey and I alone. Was this his ploy for some forced bonding? As stupid as that sounded, it had apparently worked for Jay.

"So, you and Jay survived your trip," she said.

"Yep," I said, not taking my attention off my task in the hopes that she would take a hint.

"I can't believe you forgave him," she said.

"Forgave him for what?" I asked. If I was talking to Jenna, I would be able to read between the lines. I would guess that she was talking about his general assholery throughout my formative years, but I had no idea what Jenna was talking about.

"For ruining your photographs, the night before the scholarship contest," she said. I stood and stared at her, the things in my hands forgotten. My chest tightened, squeezing until my lungs were paralyzed.

"No," was all I could say.

"But it's great that you forgave him. That was a long time ago and now Darren said you are in school for therapy or something." Her tone was so light and carefree for someone who had just stabbed me through the heart.

"No, he couldn't have. How do you know?" I asked.

"I was there. I tried to stop him, but you know, he is kind of an asshole. I would have told you sooner, but I assumed you knew," she said.

"But why?" I asked. Jay had always been a jerk to me. He had teased me and called me names, but to ruin my photographs? To ruin my chances at the art scholarship, at the life I had dreamed of? That was evil beyond what I thought he was capable of.

"I only bring it up because I worry about Darren." Either I was too shocked by the last revelation or Aubrey wasn't making sense again. I didn't want to jump to conclusions, but it was so middle school, mean girl of her to drop little bomb shells without explanation as I floundered to catch up. It left me in a constant state of turbulence and confusion.

"What does any of this have to do with Darren?" I asked, fighting back tears. I could not, under any circumstances, cry in front of Aubrey. I had to find a way to end the conversation as soon as humanly possible. I should have just turned and walked away. Fuck politeness.

"The thing you have to understand about Jay is that he likes things the way he likes things. I dated him for a long time." Something I didn't need to think about in that moment. Why was she talking to me about Jay at all? Did she somehow sense that something had happened between Jay and me? Or was she just a terrible person? Or had I misread the situation, and she genuinely cared about Darren. I didn't feel equipped to parse through Aubrey's code. "He has a way of manipulating people and situations to benefit himself. I don't know why he ruined your photography submissions. Maybe he thought he was helping me somehow, but normally his only motivation is himself, so it must have been something. I'm not saying he is an altogether bad guy. He did help Darren out after all, but I just...Darren is vulnerable right now. I would hate to see Jay step in, and steam roll the situation or use it to his own advantage. He is unpredictable."

I kept going through the motions of setting up the booth, moving as quickly as my freezing fingers and numb mind would allow. I had to be done. I had to set it up and get out of there. I had no idea what situation Aubrey was talking about, and I didn't want to ask her and look like I was out of the loop. We may not have been in high school anymore, but the rules of engagement still mattered. I couldn't entirely concede the upper ground and announce my ignorance. So instead, I would cut and run. I strung some lights, set up a mini train set with a twinkling tree, and placed out the merchandise with as much thought as my brain was capable.

"I guess my advice to you is to be careful," she said as if I had asked for her opinion. "Maybe he has changed. I know he likes to think that he has. He can have his moments, but at least in my experience, his moments were always, in the end, about getting what he wanted. And what he really wants is anyone's guess until it's too late. I tried to tell Darren all of this. I tried to warn him not to take the loan from Jay because Jay only cares about himself when it comes down to it. Darren wants to believe the best of his friend, but it's going to turn messy. I just know it. Anyone who can do what they did to you without so much as a second thought, would have no problem backstabbing his best friend. Maybe you can talk some sense into him. What he wants with Jay's money or partial ownership of your parent's store is anyone's guess."

By the time her speech had finished, the booth was mostly set up. Jay and Darren could do whatever they wanted to it. I didn't care about the sales or the booth or showing up Jay or my essay or anything at all besides getting the hell away from Aubrey, so I could try to process what she was saying.

"I can try," I said. "Well, I think I'm done here. I'm going to head back home and get warmed up. It's been a long twenty-four hours."

"I bet it has," she said with a lift off her eyebrows, as if she knew exactly what had gone down in the hotel room. And just like that, as much as I tried to stay above it, I was right back in high school trying to survive the subtle take downs of the most popular girl in school. Retelling the inter- action was impossible because it would lose the sharp sting that I felt in real life. But anyone who had ever been in an unspoken match of insults with a mean girl knew. Knew the look, the tone, the eyebrow raise and the sinking shame of not having a comeback or worse, the shame of caring so damn much.

"Yep, I gotta go," I was numb. I had to stay that way until I was behind closed doors.

"I didn't mean to upset you, Catherine," she said. "I'm just trying to help." It was the same thing she had said when she told me I smelled in freshman PE.

"Thanks," I said before turning and high tailing it out of there. She had already won. Nothing else mattered except never seeing her again. Maybe I could pack my bag. I could beg Jenna to take me in. I could run back to school and live out of my car, traveling across the country, seeing the sights. I could take Jay up on his offer to bring me to the city. With the thought of Jay, I nearly drowned.

How could I have been so damn stupid? How could I have actually believed that he liked me? That he had changed? That he gave a shit? I should have known that it was all an act. I still didn't understand what the hell he stood to gain from getting me into bed. While I knew it was stupid to trust Aubrey out right, because she too had a bad habit of being a manipulative bitch, I also couldn't argue with the evidence. It wasn't an over statement to say that he had ruined my life. He had shifted the entire trajectory I had been on. I would have won that contest. I would have gone off to study art. I could have been happy. Hot tears streamed down my face as I hurried home.

And he had been the one to give Darren a loan? What were the terms of the deal? Was sleeping with me somehow a means to an end in that? It made me sick to my stomach. My feet carried me home as my brain found a thousand reasons why I was the dumbest person to ever exist. I pushed open the door to a cold, dark, empty house. Everyone was out getting ready for the start of the holiday street fair.

It used to be my favorite time of year, now everything was awful. It was hard to see past the embarrassment and self-loathing that brought tears to my eyes, making my vision blurry. I hurried to my room, closed the door and lay on my bed, feeling very much like a teenager all over again. Would I ever be done feeling this way? Would I reach a magical point where shit rolled off my back? When I could have conversations without sounding like an idiot or replaying them again and again to scrutinize everything I said?

The worst part, by far, in all of it was the real feelings I had. Jay dancing with me. The playful teasing in the car. The coffee in the morning. The car snacks. The night. That amazing night where I thought I would simply die if I wasn't with Jay.

I had spent my whole life being carefully guarded about my feelings only to let my walls down for Jay? *For Jay?* I could have screamed. Maybe I should have gone downstairs and found my mom's wine or my dad's scotch that he kept for special occasions and drank my thoughts away, but I couldn't bring myself to do that either.

We were two days away from Christmas, then my final essay would be due. I needed to figure out my future, where I would live, what I would do. It all felt so incredibly bleak. And despite real life crashing me down, all I could think about was stupid Jay. How had it come to this?

Chapter Twenty-Seven

Somewhere in my obsessive thinking, my brain shut down, and I fell asleep. It had only been midafternoon, but I hadn't slept much the night before — don't think about that—and stress made me tired. I woke to the sound of a gentle knocking on my door. I groaned. There wasn't a single person on the planet that I would be happy to see. I didn't even think I could face Jenna because that would mean I would have to tell her everything.

The knock came again. What were the chances I could ignore it? I looked at my phone; 3pm. I hadn't slept enough. The fair was starting. The booth would be open for better or worse. For a split second, I panicked that I should be there. Then I came to my senses and thought Darren could go screw himself. He hadn't been telling me the truth since I got home.

He had allowed me to believe Mom's fantasy that he was this infallible golden child who managed to increase profits exponentially, letting me wallow in my jealousy and personal failings. He didn't warn me that Jay would be here, and then he let Jay and I go traipsing across the shoreline for chocolate, which of course ended in the worst decision of my life, only to come home and have Aubrey, of all people, drop several bombs, some of which still weren't entirely clear. No, I had a lot to be pissed off at Darren about.

"Cat." Shit. It was Jay.

"I'm not here," I said. The knob turned, and then I was sharing my cramped bedroom with Jay. He closed the door behind himself but stood close to the doorway.

"What happened?" He asked.

"Nothing happened. Why did something have to happen?" I knew I was being defensive, but I couldn't help it. I felt so exposed, so vulnerable. Part of me wanted to scream at him and another part of me needed him to get the hell away from me. I never wanted to talk to him again.

"Why did you run off from the booth? Everyone is looking for you. Aubrey said you got upset and left but wouldn't elaborate," he said.

"Of course she did. She is just so terribly concerned about me, I'm sure. You know, you two were perfect for each other. I don't know why you ever broke up," I spat out, standing up, so that Jay wasn't towering over me anymore than he normally did.

"Cat, what are you talking about?" He asked.

"I am talking about how you ruined my life!" I shouted. He took a step back as if my words were a physical force.

"What?" He asked.

"You ruined my life," I said more forcefully, shoving my pointer finger into his chest. I really wanted to wrap my fingers around his throat and squeeze. "You stole the only chance I ever had to follow my dreams. To do something that mattered to me. I hate it here! Somehow, I always get sucked right back into the bullshit of everyone else's problems, everyone else's expectations. I was trying to pick up the pieces that you left me with and be something more than the pathetic younger sister who would never be as special, or smart, or important as Darren. Only one thing ever truly made me happy. And you took it away." I felt tears streaming down my face. I wiped them away angrily.

He swallowed hard. "What are you talking about?"

"Aubrey told me what happened to my photographs," I said. I watched his face turn white. He knew exactly what I was talking about.

"Cat...I can explain," he said.

"There is nothing to explain! I wish I had never come back here. I don't need any of you. I don't need my family's approval that will never come. I need to finish school and move on," I said.

"It sounds to me like you need your family's approval a lot," he said.

"See! See! You can't help yourself. You can only pretend to care for a fraction of a second before the real you comes out," I said.

"The real me? What makes you think you know the real me?" He asked.

"You think that you have everyone else figured out, that

you are too brooding and mysterious for anyone else to understand? I know exactly who you are. You are an open goddamn book. I've always known that you were a vapid, selfish, jerk."

"That didn't seem to bother you last night," he said. I could feel his walls rebuilding just as quickly as mine had. We spent twenty-four hours together being honest and vulnerable and the first sign of trouble we were back in our corners. It felt terrible, but not at all surprising.

"You are an asshole," I said. "How can you stand here so callously knowing that you single-handedly took away everything I ever wanted?"

"You need to not let Aubrey get into your head. She is very good at that. That is why I am upset about her and Darren. Not because of some broken heart jealousy that you think. It's because she is toxic."

"This isn't about Aubrey. This is about you! It's about how you manipulated me into believing you gave a shit. It's about my pictures, my wrecked future. It's about whatever deal you made with Darren that no one felt the need to tell me about."

"Cat," he said with a long rush of breath. "All I want is to help. All I have ever wanted was to help."

"Help? Help?" I was screaming an inch away from his face. "By ruining my photos?"

"It wasn't like that," he said. "I..."

"Get out," I said. "And whatever deal you made with Darren, I will work on paying it back, so you are as far away from me and my family as possible."

"I am only supporting my friend. He came to me and told me he was stuck, so I lent him money," he said.

"What are the stipulations of this loan? What do you get out of it?"

"Nothing," he said.

"Aubrey said that there's always something in it for you," I said, feeling tears burn my eyes. I didn't want to cry in front of him, but that ship had long since sailed.

"Of course, Aubrey said that because she is a nosey bitch," he said.

"So, this is a no strings attached loan?"

"It isn't like that, Cat."

"What is it like? Explain it to me," I said, putting my hands on my hips and moving closer as if I could somehow intimidate him into giving me the answers I was looking for.

"Darren needed the money. We agreed that I would give him the money. No loan," It sounded like there was a "but" coming at the end of that thought, so I waited, staring him down, trying not to think about how his lips felt in the darkness of our bed and breakfast room. "I would have partial ownership of the store, but only so I could better finance everything and your parents could retire."

"Get out," I said, pointing toward the door.

"Cat, please," he said.

"Get out," I shouted.

He turned to go, hand on the doorknob before he stopped and turned to me.

"What do you want, Cat?" the phrase was so similar to

what he had said the night before that my cheeks flushed, and my body instantly ran warm with lust. *Stop it!* None of that.

"I want to get out of here. I want to get away from you." I couldn't stop the tears.

"That is something you don't want. What do you *want*?" He asked, emphasizing the want as my body betrayed my mind.

"I don't know," I had to admit.

"Maybe you should figure that out before you start throwing away everything you have."

"I don't have anything, thanks to you," I said.

"Maybe you do, but you are too stubborn to recognize it," Jay said. "Everyone is expecting you at the fair." With that, he turned and walked away, leaving me absolutely gutted.

Chapter Twenty-Eight

After Jay left, my phone buzzed none stop. I looked at it the first few times. Angry texts from Darren, a few from Mom, a concerned text from Jenna. That was low, getting my best friend involved.

I put it on silent and lay back in bed, wishing I could fall asleep again, but I had already taken an afternoon nap and there was no way I was falling back to sleep.

"I should finish my essay," I said, sitting up with renewed fervor. This was it. This was my chance to put all the family drama aside, sit down at my computer and type out the end of the essay I had cobbled together.

"I can always revise in editing," I said as I pulled out my little white pottery barn teen chair and opened my lap top which had been neglected for too long. My document was still opened. I was ready to type. There was no point in mourning a dream that had died a long time ago. I had a new dream now. A dream to get the hell out, for good. To prove to my family, and everyone that I could make something practical and successful of myself.

I stared at the page, rereading the last few sentences, waiting for inspiration to strike, but nothing did. My mutinous thoughts kept slipping back to Jay, and the way my heart hurt more than I thought it should. I had only been with Jay for a day. Why the hell did all of this bother me so much? True, I didn't often sleep with men casually, but still, I was an adult. I could handle a little casual sex. But it did bother me, a lot. It bothered me that I was sitting at home while my favorite part of the holiday season passed by. I used to spend the night of the fair and the party taking pictures. Everything looked even more magical through the lens of my camera. Tears burned my eyes before I shook my head.

"It was a long time ago, Cat," I told myself. Still, it hurt like a fresh wound. I couldn't help but wonder if it hurt more because it was Jay, compounded with the failing store, the loan, Aubrey somehow pulling her evil little stings in my life again. It all felt like more of a burden than I should have to carry.

Then I was right back to where I started, wondering why I cared so damn much. The answer was obvious, but I refused to admit it. It didn't matter. I would finish my essay, graduate, get a job and stay far away from the beach. Maybe I would even find a nice, respectable man, and live happily ever after. I didn't need the Christmas shop, or the long passed art show, and I certainly didn't need Jay. But even as the thought came to me, my throat closed up with emotions.

I stood from my desk and paced the room. I couldn't stay there. I got dressed into something more festive, that I hadn't been wearing for twenty-four hours and threw on my coat. I would find Jenna. That was what I needed. I had to talk to someone sane, removed from the nonsense.

The wind hit me with a harsh bite as I stepped outside. The ground was still covered in snow, but the streets and sidewalks had been cleared, which made it feel picture perfect. The smell of fires warming hearths filled the air, and if I had been in a better headspace, I would be perfectly content to enjoy the day before Christmas Eve. When I had stopped appreciating my life? When I was younger, nothing could have gotten in the way of the holiday season. Somewhere along the line, I had turned into the grinch or scrooge, only seeing the negative.

I had a plan. I would enjoy the street fair with Jenna. My essay, my uncertain future, my miserable love life—if that's even what we were calling it, my crazy family, could all wait. Still, as I got closer to the festivities, the crowded cobble streets, the twinkling lights, the brass band playing "O Come, All Ye Faithful," the Christmas tree reaching for the sky, all pulled me out of my funk despite Jay's words haunting me. *What did I want?* I thought wanting to prove my family wrong about me was enough. I thought getting out of Cape Shore was enough motivation and purpose to build a life around, but now, being back here, I was starting to doubt that. That nagging feeling that I was missing a piece of myself came into focus.

Jay had tried to do the same thing. He had tried to hang

his happiness on fulfilling the expectations of his father and the hopes of impressing his mother, and of course, that didn't work. He had been doing it his whole life, and as far as I could tell, it made him a miserable shit.

"He is a miserable shit, Cat!" I whispered to myself. "Stop feeling sympathy. He never felt any for you."

I weaved through the crowd, letting the revelry wash over me, trying to distract from the lump in my throat. I couldn't keep crying over Jay. That would be too pathetic, even for me, I had done far too much of it already. I took a different way onto the Main Street, so I could avoid the family shop and booth. I didn't need a lecture or to get pulled in to helping. And I absolutely could not face Jay.

Jenna's family's booth had a wooden frame, decorated with a pine garland and twinkling lights. They sold a limited, food truck style menu of lobster rolls (of course), fish tacos, fried chicken, and meatballs parmesan sandwiches—all of it delicious, I had no doubt.

"Hey!" It was Steve's voice. When I turned, I saw him standing behind the booth with Jenna. She served food, and he served drinks as a line snaked away from them, waiting to order.

"You guys are busy," I said, trying to keep the disappointment out of my voice. If there ever was a time I needed my best friend to ditch all her responsibilities, it was now. I sighed. She likely didn't want to be busting her ass behind the counter, but she couldn't get out of it, no matter how much I begged.

"It is unreal," Jenna said. "How's the shop doing? Darren was looking for you."

"Yeah, I heard. I haven't been there." That was all I needed to say for Jenna to suspect something was up.

"Oh," she said, narrowing her eyes. "You'll have to tell me about it later."

"I hope you have a lot of time," I said with a smirk. It was all incredibly laughable that so much had happened in the last twenty-four hours and somehow my best friend didn't know anything about it.

"I'll have to make some time," she said slowly, with lots of secret meaning.

"Text me when you are free," in between mixing drinks and passing them off to customers, Steve kept turning his gaze on us, trying to figure out what was going on. He could keep guessing because I would never tell a soul.

I wandered the Christmas fair carefully, wishing I didn't have to peek around corners and watch my back as I enjoyed the atmosphere of the holiday celebration. I probably looked like I was high on drugs or some sort of CIA agent searching for a criminal. Neither a great look. Some tiny part of me, when I had danced with Jay and spent the night with him, had hoped this fair would be drastically different. I had hoped that it would look like it had when we walked the streets of Ocean Park looking for food.

But that was a ridiculous fantasy, and I felt like a foolish child for ever having thought it. I knew who Jay was. I had always known. I couldn't believe the stupid, impulsive choices I made. I blinked away my tears. I don't know how long I walked before my phone finally buzzed.

Meet me at Lark

Be there in 5

Chapter Twenty-Nine

I turned on my heels and hurried off Main Street, leaving the street fair behind. As "Blue Christmas" done in big band brass faded behind me, I weaved through quiet side streets, mostly residential, until I came to The Lark. Inside smelled like patchouli, pine and jasmine, as I navigated the aisles filled with secondhand clothes, crystals, natural beauty products and meditation bowls situated next to spell work and candles. Off the beaten path, few people made their way to The Lark, which happened to be my go to shopping destination and fashion inspiration as a teen. Even now, walking through, I saw several things that caught my eye.

The owner was a woman my mother's age who had convinced her daughter to run it in her retirement. I felt a pang of guilt that my own mom should have been at the point of retirement, but apparently wouldn't get the opportunity unless our shop turned around, or Jay came to the rescue, apparently.

I made it to the back of the shop where little meditation pillows were set up in the corner filled with books, where Jenna already sat. The coffee place was our go to spot, but this was our secret meeting place when we couldn't be at home or on the beach.

"What's going on?" Jenna asked before I even sat. I hadn't been sure what I would tell Jenna and what I would keep private, but as soon as I started talking, the words started pouring out. I told her about Darren and Aubrey (which she already heard but listened to politely), Darren's loan, my parent's struggling business, getting chocolate with Jay and how nice he had been, and about what Aubrey had said. She took it all in, nodding and making active listening sounds.

"And," I said miserably. "I slept with Jay."

"You slept with Jay!" She shouted before covering her mouth.

"I feel like a total idiot."

"I don't think you should feel like an idiot. He is hot."

"And a horrible person."

"Really? You think Jay is just using you and your brother to get control of the shop?"

"When you put it that way, it sounds stupid. And no, that isn't what I think. I think that Jay can't help himself. He can't be involved in something and not turn it into the Jay show. Making everything about him."

"Now you agree with Aubrey?" She asked. Why was she always to reasonable?

"I don't know why you are so desperate to defend Jay. Aubrey is a bitch, but she knows Jay better than anyone," I said. "And her opinion doesn't matter. Jay sabotaged my only chance at the scholarship, and now he is micromanaging Darren and the shop into oblivion."

"I think you need to have a real conversation with all of them," she said.

"Why should I bother?" I asked. "This isn't any of my business. I don't care one way or the other what Jay does or doesn't do. My brother made his bed."

"I think you do care," she used her careful voice that she saved when she was trying to prevent Cat, the ticking time bomb, from going off.

"No, I don't care. This isn't my problem," I realized my volume was getting too loud, and I reverted back to a whisper. I didn't need October hearing my shit show of a life. "I have to finish my essay."

"Maybe there is a reason you haven't finished school," she said.

"And what reason would that be?"

"I don't know, because you don't want to," she said with a shrug.

"Why wouldn't I want to? It's all I have going for me," I said.

"Is it?"

"Yes," I said, feeling frustrated that her words mirrored Jay's.

"Alright, fine. But it does seem like you care a lot about what's happening with Darren, Jay and the store." she said. "It is easy to blame Jay. Any maybe he did fuck up your chance at a scholarship, but you are the one who chose to give up, Cat. There are more paths to a dream than one."

"You are one to talk, Jenna. You gave up on the bakery without ever trying," I said.

"Wow, that was low," she said.

"I'm sorry. I'm a terrible friend," I said. Jenna had dreamed of opening a bakery her whole life in the same way I had dreamed of being a photographer. I knew how hard following a dream could be. "I just didn't need a lecture here. Everything sucks."

"I'm sorry. I'm not trying to lecture you. I just want you to be happy, and you haven't sounded happy in a long time," she said. My stomach dropped as I thought back through our recent conversations. Did I sound unhappy? *Was I unhappy?*

"What am I supposed to do? I am stuck," I said. "I've backed myself into a corner. I spent so much time following what I thought were opportunities without ever stopping to think about what I want. Jay has been asking me for two days what I want, and it should have been an easy question, but every time I answered he poked holes in what I say, as if he knows anything about me at all. He is so infuriating. He acts like he knows everything, but he knows nothing."

"Jay was asking you what you want? Why?" she asked.

"I don't know. Why does he do anything he does? Maybe I can hide out here until the street fair is over," I said, miserably.

"I think you need to have a conversation," she said. "You can't leave with things up in the air."

"Alright," I said, but I wasn't making any promises. I wasn't entirely opposed to running far away from my problems. That was one of my talents. And maybe Jenna was right that I wasn't entirely happy, but that was just a facet of being an adult, right?

"Text me and let me know what happens," Jenna said, standing.

"Okay. Good luck with the rest of the night," I said.

"It's going to be terrible," Jenna said. "I'm not looking forward to it."

"Oh and Jenna?" I said before she was out of ear shot. "You are the most amazing baker in the world. You are going to open the best bakery Cape Shore has ever seen."

She smiled and crossed her fingers before leaving. I stayed on the meditation pillow, avoiding responsibilities. I flipped through some books about how to find yourself, which only left me rolling my eyes at the vague advice like make your bed in the morning or go for walks.

I spent as long as I could sitting in the hidden corner, watching stray shoppers walk through the store. Every so often, October walked by, asking if I or someone else needed help. I always suspected October was an interesting person, but I never really got to know her.

Eventually, I felt bad that I was camping out in her shop, so I pushed up off the floor, my butt hurting a little from sitting for an extended period of time.

When I walked out, it felt even colder than it had earlier.

I pulled my coat tight against the blustering wind, picking up flurries of snow to whip them around my face. The brass band drifted to meet my ears as I slowly walked down the sidewalk.

Chapter Thirty

I couldn't bring myself to go back to the shops, spending the rest of the evening avoiding everyone felt too heart breaking. Once again, I went to a home that felt far from welcoming. I sighed. I could have started a fire and put on a movie, but I didn't feel festive at all.

I woke the next morning to the smell of bacon, pancakes and coffee tempting me toward the kitchen until I remembered I was avoiding everyone. I pulled my door open a crack to see whose voices I could hear downstairs. "Carol of the Bells," drifted dramatically upstairs and drowned out any voices I might have heard. So I dared to step out of my door toward the bathroom when I heard Darren's voice come in a loud whisper behind his bedroom door.

"It's fine. You are my girlfriend," he said.

"It's awkward," Aubrey's voice came next. Ew. I hurried into the bathroom. It was a tie between her and Jay over who I wanted to see least. When I thought of Jay, and the way he looked at me with such utter disappointment and disdain the previous day, I felt sick to my stomach. I made my shower as long as possible before getting dressed and tip toeing downstairs, hoping everyone had cleared out.

What I saw instead was a formal breakfast around the table. With Jay, Aubrey, Darren, and my parents.

"What is going on here?" I asked, thankful that I had at least showered. Once again, I had the overwhelming desire to fuck politeness and run out of the room.

"It's Christmas Eve," Mom said, as if it was obvious.

"I'm going to take a plate to go," I said even though I would probably just grab a coffee to keep the contents of my stomach from coming back at up.

"Where were you last night?" She asked.

"I visited with Jenna then came home," I said. The room erupted in angry, outraged chatter between Darren and my parents. Aubrey and Jay both remained silent. I noticed Jay hadn't looked at me once, and I was angry at myself for being hurt over that.

"You stayed home during the fair?" Mom said.

"You should have been there with us running the booth!" Darren said. "Don't you care at all?"

"Don't accuse me of not caring, Darren! All I ever do is care too damn much. If you cared, then you would be honest with the people at this table," I said. His eyes grew wide, and his face turned ashen.

"What is she talking about, Darren?" mom said.

"What is your problem?" Darren asked, scooting his chair back so he could stand and look at me.

"What is *your* problem?" I asked.

"I didn't have a problem until you came home and tried to make everything about yourself," he said.

"What?" I asked. "Are you out of your mind?" I felt tears building behind my eyelashes. I tried to wrap myself tightly in a blanket of rage, but the hurt crept in. "I have done nothing but try to help you. But I'm done with the secrets and the nonsense. You are all crazy and dysfunctional." I made sure to point at everyone at the table.

"Me?" Aubrey said innocently. "I was only trying to help."

Both Jay and I turned a fiery gaze on her. At least we were united in something. "Stay out of it, Aubrey," Jay said.

"She's the one who pointed at me!" She said.

"Please leave my girlfriend out of this. You need to get over high school eventually, Cat," Darren said.

"Get over high school?" What a dismissive thing to say. It made me wonder if he knew that Jay had ruined my pictures. Or maybe he did, but he was too self-involved to care.

"Darren, what did Catherine want you to tell us?" Mom asked while dad looked between all of us as if watching a daytime soap, shoveling pancakes and bacon in his mouth.

"Nothing, mom," Darren practically shouted.

"It's not nothing. I have wallowed in public failure several times. It is time for you to experience just a little bit. Besides, we can help you," I said. "Mom and Dad would still think you are a golden boy even if you shoveled shit for a living."

"Catherine, don't be so dramatic. You know we love you," Mom said.

"Sure, just not as much as Darren," I said.

"That is very childish. It isn't a competition," she said.

"Isn't it?" I asked. "You sure as hell made it feel that way."

"Don't be silly, Catherine," she said. I looked around the room in disbelief. Either they were all out of their mind or I was. There were no other explanations for the absolute insanity that happened when we all got together.

"Darren, tell her." I said with absolute finality.

"You just want me to be the fuck up instead of you," he said. "We all know you extended your final course. Was it because you failed the first time around?"

"I don't give a shit. After this week, I am leaving, with or without a degree. I can't stay. There is nothing here for me," I said, swallowing back overwhelming emotions. I had thought very briefly that maybe there was something here for me. I trained my eyes on Darren, so they wouldn't stray to Jay. "But your whole life is here. You have to be honest and face this problem head on. Everyone likes to pretend that I am childish, but you haven't dealt with real adversity once. It's time."

The room was silent as Darren looked around. Aubrey was shaking her head no. While Jay stared at the table, and my parents looked worriedly at Darren.

"I borrowed too much money," he said finally. "I tried to grow too much too fast and I owe more money than we are set to make back. I borrowed money from Jay to cover the bank loan."

"Oh Darren," Mom said, hands to mouth in shock and horror that her baby had royal fucked up. "How did this happen? We trusted you."

"I am fixing it, Mom. I didn't want you to have to worry. The shop and the booth did amazing last night. We are going to recover," he said. I felt awful. He looked so sad and dejected.

"I just can't believe this. I mean, you have always been so responsible. Maybe Catherine, but not you," Mom said, and I officially had enough.

"Jesus, mom. What the hell? All my life, you have treated me like a second-class citizen. You have doted on Darren like he could do no wrong, and in the end it hurt both of us. Darren has to live up to unreasonable expectations, and I have to fight every second of my life for someone to give me any credit for my accomplishments. You need to get over it. And Darren, I love you. You fucked up, but it isn't anything you can't handle. I believe in you. But, your girlfriend and best friend are terrible people. Aubrey's life mission in school was to make my life a living hell. And Jay ruined my photos for the scholarship contest. He is the reason I am a psychologist major. You need to make better choices."

I turned to leave when the doorbell rang. The room fell into a tense silence.

"Alright, I guess I'll go get it," I said. My nerves vibrated with spent adrenaline as I walked through the living room and pulled open the front door to see Steve standing there.

"Oh, hi," I said, completely unprepared to act like a normal person after all the yelling.

"Hey," he said with a big smile, holding out a rose. I stared at his out stretched hand, trying to make sense of it. I heard commotion behind me, and when I turned to look, I saw everyone crowded in the doorway to see who had rung the bell.

"Steve?" Aubrey said with derision.

"Hey Steve," Darren said in a friendly tone, while Jay's expression only looked dangerously dark.

"Hi," Steve said. I could tell that he was suddenly self-conscious with the audience. He shoved the rose closer to me.

"Oh, thanks," I said, taking it to spare him from utter humiliation, although I had no interest in a rose, certainly not from Steve.

"I didn't have your number," he said. "So, I thought I'd stop by to see if you wanted to go to the Christmas party tonight."

"Oh right," I said. I had completely forgotten that life continued outside the drama and utter upheaval happening inside the four walls of my childhood home. "Um, sure." I said.

"Steve, it's so nice to see you! Do you want some break-fast?" My mom asked, breaking away from the group to usher Steve inside. She wasn't oblivious to the tension that existed between all of us, but that's what my mom did. She ignored things and brushed it under the rug, so no one had to face it directly.

"Mom, I'm sure Steve has somewhere to be," I said. I had just agreed to go to the party with him, again to save his feelings—I really had to stop doing that—but I didn't want to have breakfast with him. I had been just about to storm out of the room.

"No, I don't," Steve said. "Breakfast sounds great Mrs. Lane."

"Wonderful!" She wrapped her arm around Steve and brought him further into the house.

We all had no choice but to turn and followed them. I moved as slowly as I could. Jay also hung back.

"Are you really going out with him?" Jay whispered. I stopped and looked at him. Everyone else had made it to the dining room while Jay, and I lingered in the living room.

"What do you care?" I asked.

"You know why I care," he said, closing the space between us. My eyes darted to his lips before I remembered that I hated his guts. I wished I could forget the way his hands had felt on my body.

"Nope, I can't possibly imagine why you would care. And Yes, I am going with him. He's a nice guy," I said.

"Don't," Jay said.

"It's cute that you think I give a shit about your opinion," I said, walking toward the dining room. "If it were up to me, Jay, I would never, ever see you again."

"Cat," he said, trying to grab my arm, which I pulled away with a glare, leaving him alone in the living room.

Chapter Thirty-One

Back in the dining room, someone had pulled up an extra chair for Steve, who was happily filling his plate with breakfast. Everyone but him and my mother looked miserable. Even my dad didn't look all that thrilled to have a newcomer at the table.

Once again, propriety dictated that I sit and eat, but somehow my spot ended up between Jay and Steve. I hoped Jay wouldn't return, but of course, I was never that lucky. He sat down beside me, his elbow bumping mine as he reached for the bacon.

"Watch your elbow," I said.

"You watch yours."

"You were the one moving. It is your job to be more careful," I said.

"Well, if you don't want your elbow bumped, you need to be mindful of mine."

"That isn't how it works," I said, my anger rising. Why was he always like this?

"It is if I don't watch my elbow. Then you don't have a choice but to watch your own."

"So, Steve, what have you been up to?" Mom asked, trying to redirect the conversation and pull the attention away from mine and Jay's pointless squabble.

"Oh, just bartending. I graduated last spring with a communications degree, but I haven't really decided what to do with that yet, so I'm just trying to get some money in the bank," he said.

"How's the market for communications jobs?" Jay asked without any emotion behind his voice.

"Eh, not great. I thought I wanted to be a journalist, but you know, newspapers are dying, so who knows?" he said.

"Sounds like you'll be bartending for a while," Jay said in typical Jay fashion. He couldn't help but shit on everyone around him.

"Not everyone can be a miserable, big city, hot shot," I said.

"Not everyone can put the responsibility of their failure on someone else's shoulders," Jay said. I nearly gasped at the low blow.

"Wow, that's some strong gaslighting there," I said. I blinked fast to keep the tears at bay. I knew the whole table was looking at us. I didn't want to storm away in defeat, but I couldn't stay there anymore. I pushed away from the table.

"Are we still on for tonight?" Steve asked.

"She'll be fine. She's always been kind of dramatic like

that," Aubrey said with a smile. I was tempted to deck her right in the face, but instead I just went to my room.

After having a good, ugly cry, I sat at my desk. I had to finish my essay. I needed a way out, a path forward, some sort of future. Even if it wasn't perfect, it was better than being stuck under my brother's shadow forever.

I paused every few words to brush tears away and feel sorry for myself. By the time the sun started to set, I had finished my essay. I didn't know if it was good enough to pass the class, but it was done. I closed my computer and turned my attention to getting ready for the Christmas party.

I opened my closet, sliding the hangers from one side to the other, trying to decide what aesthetic I should aim for. I had no interest in Steve. He was a nice guy, but there was no spark. Maybe waiting for a spark was stupid, especially since the only spark I had ever felt was with Jay, of all people. I should put something boring on like jeans and a red cable knit, so as not to give Steve any ideas of this being a real date. But Jay would be there, so slinky red dress it was. I had my doubts that he ever gave a shit about me at all, but if I could make him turn his head just once, maybe that would be enough vindication that there was some small regret for being himself and making me cry so much.

When the doorbell rang for the second time, I walked down feeling self-conscious in my dress. I had bought it for a previous Christmas party one year when I was feeling adventurous, but ended up chickening out of wearing it. When I came to the landing, I saw Jay had already opened the door.

"Your date is here," he said with a tone that could have been disgust or mocking or both.

"Thanks so much," I said with a wink. He stared at me with intense eyes, trying to communicate something that I wasn't going to decipher.

"Ready?" I asked Steve, as I grabbed my coat from the hook.

"You look amazing," he said. I spared one last glance at Jay as we walked out the door. His eyes were clouded with darkness as I shut the door in his face.

"What's up between you and Jay?" Steve asked as we walked toward town, choosing the last topic that I wanted to talk about.

"Nothing," I said.

"Doesn't seem like nothing. You guys seemed friendly at the bar and now it seemed like you want to kill each other."

"Well, maybe I do. But let's not talk about Jay," I said, but then I couldn't think of anything else to talk about, so we walked in silence.

"How come you haven't been home since high school?" He asked. Wow, he was 0 for two on the topic choices.

"I've just been busy," I said, not sure why I lied.

"Gonna be a big shot psychologist huh?" He asked.

"Yep, I'll be able to psychoanalyze all your problems," I said. "I'll even give you a discount."

"Cool," he said. My eyebrows furrowed as I looked sideways at him. Did he think I was serious? And maybe the more important question was, did he think I was serious about being *his* therapist—a big ethical no, no—or about a discount? Weird. This was going to be a long night. By the time we got to the Community Hall, I regretted wearing the dress for the thirty seconds that Jay had to drool over it. I was freezing.

Steve pulled open the door for me, and we stepped inside, instantly transported to a winter wonderland. The band played "Silent Night," and my heart nearly exploded with hurt as I thought of mine and Jay's dance. I was so pathetic. Pining over a man that had been so awful to me. I wouldn't cry. I wouldn't cry. I wouldn't cry.

The community hall was done in golds, reds, and greens. With lighted tinsel garlands running the length of the crown molding, Christmas trees in every corner, and giant ornaments hanging from the ceiling. The Christmas committee had really out done themselves. At the far end, there was a raised stage with a band and a dance floor in front. Food and drinks were set up at various tables around the room along with face paint-ing, Santa, and "reindeer" petting, which was really just dogs with antlers, for the kids. All in all, it was always an amazing time. Only this year, I was struggling not to cry like an idiot.

We checked our coat and moved further into the hall before Steve turned to me.

"Want to dance?" Steve asked.

"Sure," I said. Thankfully, the song had changed to "Holy Night," but when Steve wrapped his arms around me, I felt nothing. I plastered on a fake smile, which I worried was just my lips pulling up in a disingenuous grin. Steve, for his part, seemed completely oblivious, which I supposed was good. He didn't have to be the love of my life for us to have a nice evening. We circled around like two kids at an awkward middle school dance.

When the song was over, we got a drink, then grabbed a bite to eat and watched the kids petting the dogs.

"I wonder if they would let me pet the dogs," I said.

"I think it's for kids," he said.

"Right," I said. I was bored. This "date" wasn't nearly distracting enough. I found my gaze moving over the room every few minutes to see if Jay had arrived, not sure what I would do if I did see him, but I just had to know if he was nearby.

I followed Steve around the room from one activity to the next, saying hello to everyone I recognized, which was a lot of people, all asking why I hadn't finished school yet. By the time we stopped in a corner for a breather, I felt mentally drained.

Then Jay walked in. I didn't know if he saw me or not, but my eyes followed him through the room until he was lost in the crowd. Part of me wished he would come over and talk to me, even if it was just to throw insults around.

"This is nice," Steve said. When I turned, I realized he was standing very close. My eyes grew wide as I instinctively pulled back. I did not want to kiss Steve. I did not want to kiss Steve. All I could think about was the feel of Jay's lips on mine, and although I could never forgive him, or feel those lips ever again, I wasn't ready to move on.

"Steve, I..." I didn't know how I would finish that

sentence because Darren interrupted me. It was the first time I was that happy to see him since I got home.

"Cat, can I talk to you?" Darren asked, pulling me away from Steve in the nick of time.

"Sure," I said too quickly, walking away from Steve to follow Darren through the Christmasy halls that branched out from the main room. "What's up?"

"First, I want to say I'm sorry. I've been a real jerk. I've let me own stress cloud my judgement. The shop isn't your responsibility, and I really appreciate your help," he said.

I looked around. "Okay, where is my brother?" I said.

He laughed. "But..."

"Oh alright, here it comes," I said with a smile.

"You are being an impulsive ass," he said.

"Excuse me?" I said.

"Jay has been in love with you since he met you in the first grade," he said. I tripped over my own feet and nearly face planted on the marble floor.

"You are so full of it," I said.

"I'm not. He assumed you hated him, and that he would never have a chance. Don't get me wrong. He is also an idiot. The two of you are idiots together. You've spent so long looking for happiness everywhere but right here," he said.

"I don't believe you," I said. "Why are you doing this?"

"Because I can't keep watching you throw your life away," he said.

"I'm not throwing my life away. I finally finished my essay. Everything is fine," I said.

"You can lie to yourself, but you can't lie to me, Cat.

Think about what I said." He turned abruptly and walked away. I realized that we had ended up in another room in the community building. When I stopped and took a good look around, I gasped.

"What the..." I said, trying to make sense of it. Around me, on every available wall, were photographs. Not just any photographs. My photographs. All the pictures I had taken from the time I first got a camera and discovered the dark room to the moment I put it away for good. People milled about, admiring them. I hadn't seen my own work in four years when I locked it all in the back of a closet to collect dust. What the hell was going on?

Chapter Thirty-Two

I let my fingers lightly graze the frames as I walked the perimeter of the room, tears of happiness—for once—slipping from my eyes. My heart felt suddenly so full to see my work on display that I couldn't believe I had ignored it for so long.

"Cat," it was Jay's voice.

"Did you do this?" I asked, looking at him.

He nodded. "I know you hate me. And I don't blame you. You have every right to hate me. I was a dick. I treated you like shit because I didn't know how else to get your attention, and I knew that you were way too cool for me. You have always been the most amazing woman I have ever known. You are unique and surprising and weird and creative and funny, and I am only ever happy when you are nearby.

"I was there the night your painting was ruined. I think Aubrey suspected all along that I was in love with you. She hated you because of me. My biggest regret is ever dating her, but once again, I let other people's expectations dictate my behavior. I dated her because I thought my dad would appreciate it. I thought the other kids at school expected me to. Who turns down the most popular girl without good reason? It was really stupid. But she was jealous. She wanted to win the contest even though she had no interest in pursuing art.

"She planned to sabotage your photo with the spray bleach. When I tried to grab it from her, it accidentally splashed all over your submissions. I have regretted it ever since, but I couldn't say anything, or you would have hated me even more than you already did.

"Please don't let your vision, talent and dreams go because of what happened four years ago. You don't ever have to talk to me again, but please, take a chance on yourself," he said with tears glistening in his eyes. I didn't think Jay was capable of crying. "This is Charles Wagner." Jay walked us to an older gentleman wearing a tailored suit. "He is a curator for an art dealership in New York. When I sent him your work, he was very interested. You two should talk."

Then he walked away as my brain tried to catch up.

"Catherine," Charles Wagner said, holding out his hand. "It's nice to meet you. I love your work."

"Thank you," I said, numb and confused, unsure how to even respond.

"You have a unique perspective that I think would fit in well with our gallery," he said. Holy shit, was this really happening? *Wait, where was Jay going?* I thought. It was a stupid thought, but I was slowly catching up to everything that Jay had said. He hadn't sabotaged my photographs. I believed him. He had always been in love with me.

"That would be amazing," I said, "but can you just excuse me for one minute?"

"I...um..." I didn't let him finish his thought before I hurried out of the gallery into the main party. The band played "Last Christmas," as people danced, ate, drank and mingled. I couldn't see Jay anywhere. I had to find him. I couldn't wait another second without telling him how I felt. Tears fell down my face.

"Cat, you okay?" Jenna asked, grabbing my shoulders.

"Have you seen Jay? I have to find him," I said.

"What's going on?" She asked.

"I've been so stupid. I just have to talk to him," I said.

"I thought he was leaving," she said. I pulled from her grip and ran for the door, my heels threatening to break my neck. I pushed open the door. The street was empty save for a lone figure walking the middle of the cobble stones, hands in pocket, head dipped down in the spotlight of the full moon and the twinkling Christmas lights.

"Jay," I shouted. He paused and turned. I ran for him, my heel catching on one of the cobble stones, spilling me forward. Before I hit the ground, his thick arms caught me.

"What's going on? Why aren't you talking to the curator?" He asked.

"I will. I just..." Now that I was there, wrapped in his warm embrace, looking up into his stony, but sincere face, I had no idea what to say. I swallowed hard. "I...I've been so stupid. I just, I've spent my whole life trying to find my place, and I guess I never realized that it was here all along. I should have known sooner." Before I could finish my thought, his lips were pressed to mine.

"It's okay, Kitty Cat. I know," he said. I grabbed the collar of his coat, pulled him close and kissed him hard.

Epilogue

I woke on Christmas morning with Jay's arm draped over my stomach and the length of my back pressed tightly against his body. I couldn't help but smile. *Holy Shit, this is real,* I thought to myself, and I couldn't be happier.

After finding Jay, he had texted the art dealer that we would discuss the details of an acquisition of my pieces in the morning before he took me back home for probably the greatest night of my life. I didn't know for certain what my future held, but I knew it didn't involve psychology. Jay had convinced me, and conveniently set up the means, for me to not give up on my dream. He and Jenna had been right though. I should have been pursuing it all along regardless of the contest.

Still, I couldn't wait to dig out my camera and start taking pictures again. I hoped that my paper was good enough to afford me a passing grade and a degree, so all that time wasn't wasted, but my real plan was to sell photos in the shop and maybe set up my own gallery.

"Morning." Jay's voice reverberated through my body, pulling me from my thoughts.

"Morning," I said, remembering the awkwardness of the last time we had woken up together. This time I just felt butterflies in my stomach. "I can't believe this happened."

"It's all I ever wanted," he said. I took slow deep breaths, so I didn't get overly emotional while lying in my small twin sized bed with Jay, our bodies pressed impossibly close.

"I decided I'm not going back to school," I said. "I'm staying here. You've been right all along."

"I know," he said.

"So humble," I said. "I'm gonna dip into savings and get an apartment as I try to get this photography thing up off the ground. I could open a studio, do portraits and weddings and sell my prints. I'm pretty excited."

"You don't need to dip into your savings."

"I know that everything is all sunshine and roses at the moment, but I don't think it will stay that way if I live at home past this week," I said. Even as I said it, I couldn't wait to get my own apartment in my perfect little beach town that I had missed so much. There had been a hole in my soul ever since I put my camera away and left Cape Shore. Now I felt so full, I might just burst.

"I'll get a place," he said. I sat up and turned to look at him, pulling up the sheet to cover my naked chest.

"You mean?" I couldn't finish the question for fear of embarrassing myself with overly ambitious, wishful thinking.

"I told you; I am only happy when I am with you," he said. "I will never let you go again."

"What about your work in the city?" I asked.

"It's the future Cat. I'll work from home," he said. Tears filled my eyes as I nodded, not trusting myself to speak. He brushed the tear from my cheek with his thick, calloused thumb and pulled me in for a deep kiss.

I realized that I would have to announce our relationship sooner rather than later, but that could wait. I wanted to bask in the greatest Christmas gift I had ever gotten for as long as possible.

Thank you!

Thank you for reading Back Home For Christmas! If you enjoyed this book, please consider rating it on Amazon, Goodreads or wherever you buy your books!

For a FREE SPICY bonus chapter visit:
www.amberreedromance.com

About the Author

Amber Reed is an author of contemporary romance. Her favorite tropes include, enemies to lovers, forced proximity, fake dating and more. When she is not writing she is spending time reading, crafting, doing yoga, playing with her three cats & spending time with her family. Visit her at **www.amberreedromance.com** to get the latest news on new releases!

tiktok.com/@amber.reed.romance

instagram.com/ambriswritng

facebook.com/amberreedauthor

Printed in Great Britain
by Amazon